"The Next Wakes Up, Y Even If I'm Up.

"You figure we're going to come to fists over him?" Cassie whispered, a smile in her voice as they both leaned over the crib.

She was barely a foot away. A sliver of light from the hall illuminated her face. He inched closer. Her gaze dropped to his mouth and lingered. He wanted to put his palms along her face, bring her close, touch his lips to hers. Slip his hands under her pajama top, feel her skin—

She straightened abruptly. "I don't— I mean…"

He pulled back. "Right. Yes. Of course." What the hell was he doing?

"I'll see you later," she said, then hurried off ahead of him.

When he went to bed a few minutes later, he noticed her bedroom light was still on. He stood outside her door for a few seconds in case she called out to him.

She didn't, and he went into his increasingly lonely bedroom, wondering at all the changes in his life and what would come next. He was ready for the next adventure.

Dear Reader,

This May, Silhouette Desire's sensational lineup starts with Nalini Singh's *Awaken the Senses*. This DYNASTIES: THE ASHTONS title is a tale of sexual awakening starring one seductive Frenchman. (Can you say ooh-la-la?) Also for your enjoyment this month is the launch of Maureen Child's trilogy. The THREE-WAY WAGER series focuses on the Reilly brothers, triplets who bet each other they can stay celibate for ninety days. But wait until brother number one is reunited with *The Tempting Mrs. Reilly*.

Susan Crosby's BEHIND CLOSED DOORS series continues with *Heart of the Raven,* a gothic-toned story of a man whose self-imposed seclusion has cut him off from love…until a sultry woman, and a beautiful baby, open up his heart. Brenda Jackson is back this month with a new Westmoreland story, in *Jared's Counterfeit Fiancée,* the tale of a fake engagement that leads to real passion. Don't miss Cathleen Galitz's *Only Skin Deep,* a delightful transformation story in which a shy girl finally falls into bed with the man she's always dreamed about. And rounding out the month is *Bedroom Secrets* by Michelle Celmer, featuring a hero to die for.

Thanks for choosing Silhouette Desire, where we strive to bring you the best in smart, sensual romances. And in the months to come look for a new installment of our TEXAS CATTLEMAN'S CLUB continuity and a brand-new TANNERS OF TEXAS title from the incomparable Peggy Moreland.

Happy reading!

Melissa Jeglinski

Melissa Jeglinski
Senior Editor
Silhouette Books

Please address questions and book requests to:
Silhouette Reader Service
U.S.: 3010 Walden Ave., P.O. Box 1325, Buffalo, NY 14269
Canadian: P.O. Box 609, Fort Erie, Ont. L2A 5X3

HEART OF THE RAVEN

SUSAN CROSBY

Silhouette® Desire

Published by Silhouette Books

America's Publisher of Contemporary Romance

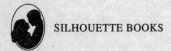 SILHOUETTE BOOKS

ISBN 0-373-76653-X

HEART OF THE RAVEN

Copyright © 2005 by Susan Bova Crosby

This edition published by arrangement with Harlequin Books S.A.

® and TM are trademarks of Harlequin Books S.A., used under license.
Trademarks indicated with ® are registered in the United States Patent
and Trademark Office, the Canadian Trade Marks Office and in other
countries.

Visit Silhouette Books at www.eHarlequin.com

Printed in U.S.A.

Books by Susan Crosby

Silhouette Desire

The Mating Game #888
Almost a Honeymoon #952
Baby Fever #1018
Wedding Fever #1061
Marriage on His Mind #1108
Bride Candidate #9 #1131
*His Most Scandalous Secret #1158
*His Seductive Revenge #1162
*His Ultimate Temptation #1186
The Groom's Revenge #1214
The Baby Gift #1301
†Christmas Bonus, Strings Attached #1554
†Private Indiscretions #1570
†Hot Contact #1590
†Rules of Attraction #1647
†Heart of the Raven #1653

*The Lone Wolves
†Behind Closed Doors

SUSAN CROSBY

believes in the value of setting goals, but also in the magic of making wishes. A longtime reader of romance novels, Susan earned a B.A. in English while raising her sons. She lives in the central valley of California, the land of wine grapes, asparagus and almonds. Her checkered past includes jobs as a synchronized swimming instructor, personnel interviewer at a toy factory and trucking company manager, but her current occupation as a writer is her all-time favorite.

Susan enjoys writing about people who take a chance on love, sometimes against all odds. She loves warm, strong heroes; good-hearted, self-reliant heroines…and happy endings.

Susan loves to hear from readers. You can visit her at her Web site, www.susancrosby.com.

One

Cassie Miranda shivered as she maneuvered her car up a steep, bumpy driveway on Wolfback Ridge. She hunched over the steering wheel to study her surroundings through the windshield. Downright eerie, she thought, slowing to a crawl. What happened to the blue sky and balmy weather that had followed her across the Golden Gate Bridge to Sausalito?

Until a minute ago the gorgeous September day would've had photographers racing around the city to take postcard-perfect pictures and businessmen ditching work for the Giants' game. Then, without warning, gloom had blanketed the sky, as if a thundercloud hovered over just this piece of property. She glanced at her rearview mirror. Sure enough, still an azure sky behind her and a slice of San Francisco Bay.

The house came into view, a soaring glass-and-wood structure with a spectacular view of the San Francisco skyline and the world's most famous bridge—if only the view hadn't been blocked by the untended forest surrounding the property. She swore no ray of sunshine could penetrate the foliage. Her new client obviously required an abnormal amount of privacy.

She didn't mind eccentric—to a point. If she'd wanted everyday-run-of-the-mill all the time, she wouldn't have chosen to be a private investigator.

Cassie parked under a gnarly tree that looked to be a century old. A city girl all her life, she guessed it was an oak, but the only thing she knew about oaks was that acorns grew on them. She didn't see any acorns.

She grabbed her briefcase and leather jacket from the passenger seat and climbed out of the car. It was quiet. Too quiet. As if birds were afraid to be there.

Cassie made a slow sweep of the terrain with her gaze as she slipped into her jacket. Chills tiptoed down her spine. Someone was watching her.

"It was a dark and stormy night," she muttered, figuring if she spoke the hackneyed phrase aloud it would make her laugh. It didn't.

She pulled her braid free of the jacket and let it fall against her spine. The lack of birdsong made her wonder if a wild animal was crouched nearby, watching her. Stalking her. That would scare the birds into silence, wouldn't it? A wolf, perhaps? Is that why this place was named Wolfback Ridge—because wolves ran free?

She scanned the property again, admired the hand-carved sign that said *Raven's View*, then lifted her gaze to the house. Tinted windows. Was it the client watching her? He even *sounded* gothic—Heath Raven. The name alone gave her an image of him. Dark and mysterious, maybe even disfigured. Tormented.

Cassie shook off her overactive imagination. One of her Los Angeles bosses had assigned her the case, a missing person. She'd called the client immediately and set up an appointment to see him, even though it was lunchtime. He'd sounded normal. A quick Internet search yielded the information that he was an architect, a highly acclaimed one. How bizarre could he be?

She walked toward the house, her boots crunching gravel along the rustic path leading to the building. The sky turned inky as the structure itself blocked the only remaining hope of sun creeping in.

Cassie trusted her instincts, and her instincts were screaming at her to turn tail and run, that the man who lived in this dreary setting was going to make her personal demons surface, ones she'd buried deep and long ago. But just then the big wooden door opened and a man stood framed in the doorway.

He wasn't disfigured. Other than that, she'd nailed him. Dark brown hair overdue for a trim, angular features, clear green eyes, assessing and, yes, tormented. A too-thin body, but solid, too.

"Ms. Miranda?" he asked in that perfectly normal voice but without the slightest smile in his eyes.

"Yes. Good afternoon." She passed him her business card, which identified her as Cassie Miranda of ARC Security & Investigations.

"I'm Heath Raven," he said, taking a step back. "Please come in."

He wore blue jeans and a red polo shirt, more normalcy.

Yet nothing seemed normal at all.

The house was as silent as a padded cell. The sleek furnishings of the living room they stepped into looked unused, as did the fireplace, which showed no signs of ever having been lit. The huge windows should've allowed light to flood in. Instead it was dim. Dismal. And sad—especially sad, as if the house was in mourning.

Cassie pulled a notebook and pen from her pocket as she sat on the sofa. He stood a distance away.

"Who's missing, Mr. Raven?" she asked.

His jaw hardened. "My child. My child is missing."

His words hit hard, a blow to the stomach. This wasn't a case for her firm, but for the P.D. She closed her notebook. "What do the police say?"

He shook his head.

"I don't understand. A child who disappears—"

"The woman who is carrying my child disappeared. She left a note. The police won't get involved because she went voluntarily."

Anger coated his words—at the woman or the police? Understandable, either way.

"May I see the note?" she asked.

He left the room, giving her a chance to catch her breath. If she'd known there was a child involved… No. She would've met with him regardless. She just wished she'd been prepared. Any case involving a child kept her up at night, drove her to exhaustion. She pushed harder for answers, demanded more of herself and everyone around her.

"Here," he said, handing her a single sheet of pink stationery.

Dear Heath,
     I need to figure things out. Don't try to find me. I'll be in touch later.
     Eva

Not exactly a love letter, Cassie thought. "When did you receive this?"

"It came in the mail this morning."

"Is she your wife?"

"No. We had a one-night stand over eight months ago. I offered to marry her, several times, but she said no. Several times." He walked away from her.

"Why would she leave?"

He looked back sharply. "I didn't abuse her, if that's what you're thinking."

"I'm gathering facts. That's what I do."

Impatience surfacing, he dragged his hands down his face. "Here's the story," he said. "I don't get out much. Most of the time people come to me when I need something. Eva works as a clerk in my lawyer's office, and she was assigned to bring me paperwork to read and sign. After almost a year of seeing her once a week or so, we slept together. Once. She got pregnant."

"When is she due?"

"In three weeks." He moved around the room again, not stopping to touch anything, just moving, pacing. Prowling.

"Are you sure the child is yours?"

He hesitated a fraction of a second. "I have no reason to believe otherwise."

She measured his response and decided if he'd questioned the issue before, it was settled in his mind—or almost so. He'd be a fool not to have some doubt, based on what he'd told her. "Okay. Were there any clues that she was about to take off?"

He came to an abrupt halt. "None." The harshly uttered word conveyed all of his brimming emotions. "She stops by every few days. She gives me an update from her latest doctor's appointment, we talk a little, and that's it. I've never done anything to make her run away. She agreed to shared custody as soon as the child was weaned. We have an amicable relationship."

An amicable relationship? Cassie thought it was an odd description, implying they were not friends but merely acquaintances.

"Do you give her money?" she asked.

"Yes."

She waited. He didn't expand on his answer.

"I'm going to need more detail than that."

"Ms. Miranda. Eva is carrying my child. I want my child well taken care of. That starts in the womb. Short of Eva moving in here, which she refused to do, I thought that making her life easier with some extra money would only help. I will show you the accounting of my payments to her, but what does it matter?"

"It matters because it establishes a pattern. Maybe she ran off and is holding your unborn child hostage because she wants more money." Cassie tapped her pen against the pad she'd opened again. "She says she'll be in touch. Why aren't you just waiting her out? If you trusted her, you would do what she asked."

He looked away, his hands clenching and unclenching, shoulders stiff. The barely contained emotion fascinated her. Still waters ran very deep.

"Three years ago my son died. My only child," he said, then faced her again. "I won't lose this child, too."

His pain pierced the room like a siren's wail. Cassie's heart opened wide with sympathy. She was twenty-nine years old, and she'd seen suffering and endured a lot in her own life, but nothing like losing a child.

Her suffering— No, she wouldn't dwell. "I'll help you," she said to Heath finally.

His relief brought quiet back into the room. "Thank you."

"What do you think she meant in her note when she said she needed to figure things out?"

He straightened, focusing on her, on the new direction of questioning, as she had intended.

"I have no idea."

"Did she have a boyfriend?"

"Not that I'm aware of."

"What about family?"

"She was vague about it. She spoke of her parents and that they live 'back east,' but that was all."

"Okay. It's something to start with. I'll need more information. Her last name, address. Anything else you can give me."

He nodded. "Let's go to my office."

She followed him up a massive staircase and into a large workroom. Her gaze didn't linger on the two substantial tables with blueprints spread on them, or on the unusual pieces of oversize computer equipment she guessed were necessary to being an architect.

Her attention fixed on the fact the entire outside wall of the room was windows. And every window was covered by blinds. And every blind was closed.

Heath appreciated the efficiency with which Cassie worked. Even before she'd started asking questions he'd guessed she was detail oriented. Her starched-and-pressed white shirt and crisp Wranglers told him she was meticulous and that the little things mattered.

She was also a jumble of energy. She moved fast, thought fast, yet was deliberate. He couldn't give himself credit for choosing the right investigator, because he'd actually been referred to her boss, Quinn Gerard. Gerard was out of town when Heath called. Cassie was at her desk. Simple as that.

She had presence. Her pointed-toe cowboy boots brought her within a few inches of his six foot one. Her golden-brown hair hung in a thick braid to her waist. Her dark blue eyes could be penetrating or sympathetic. She already seemed to know when to divert him, to make him stop focusing on his anger—his fury—that Eva had taken off. He figured he could work fine with Cassie.

At the moment she was writing in her notebook. She'd taken off her old and apparently cherished leather jacket and hung it neatly on the back of a chair. At her waist was a holstered gun. He hadn't expected that. He didn't know why he was surprised, but he acknowledged it as sexist. If Quinn Gerard had shown up for the job, Heath wouldn't have been surprised at the weapon.

"What kind of gun is that?" he asked.

She didn't look up. "Sig Sauer. Forty caliber."

"Are you good with it?"

"Is San Francisco foggy?" She smiled at him, her confidence more than a little appealing to him.

"I don't always carry, but I didn't know what I was walking into today. Okay—" she tapped her pen on her notebook "—you said Eva works at your lawyer's office."

"She did. She went on maternity leave starting last week."

She frowned. "That's early, isn't it? It seems like women work until their water breaks these days."

"I wouldn't know." His ex-wife had stopped working the day they were married, which had been fine with him.

"Is it a big firm?"

"Torrance and Torrance."

"That's a big firm," she stated. "I worked for Oberman, Steele and Jenkins for five years as an in-house investigator, so I know a lot of the law firms. OSJ does criminal work, and T and T does corporate, but they must operate alike. She would have friends at work—other clerks and paralegals. In a company with that many employees, there would be at least one or two she would go to lunch with. I'll check it out."

Heath braced his legs. "You can't," he said to her back.

"I can't what?"

"Talk to anyone at the office."

She looked at him as if he'd lost his mind. "I have to."

"You can't."

"Why?"

"Because our relationship was secret. They have a strict no-fraternization-with-the-clients rule. She would be fired."

"No one knows you're the father?"

"No one at her work, at least."

"I wonder how she managed that." Her toe tapped the floor. "It would be very hard to keep that sort of thing to yourself."

"She likes her job. She wants to hold on to it."

"Hmm." After a few seconds she flipped a page. "We'll skip that for now. Current residence?"

He passed her a card he'd pulled from his Rolodex file. She wrote down the address.

"She has a roommate," he said. "Darcy. I don't know her last name."

"Have you been to the apartment?"

"No."

"So, the one-night-stand thing really was all there was to it? You never went on a date?"

"Never." Admitting it out loud made it seem sordid. It hadn't been sordid. He hadn't taken advantage of Eva. She'd been willing. More than willing. If anything, she'd come after him.

Cassie looked at the Rolodex card again. "Is this her current phone number?"

"Yes. It's a cell."

"I take it you've tried to reach her."

"It's turned off."

"Okay." She wrote down the number and gave him back the card. "Friends she's talked about?"

"Someone named Megan. A guy named Jay."

"In what context did she discuss them?"

"They were people she went out with after work and on the weekends."

"You don't think this Jay could be a boyfriend?"

"Didn't sound like it." Heath liked the way she fired questions, hardly waiting for his answer. Thinking one step ahead.

"You mentioned parents 'back east.' She never said their names?"

"No."

"Any mention of siblings?"

"A sister, Tricia. Older. She has three children. Eva called her for pregnancy advice. Said she couldn't talk to anyone else."

"Is she local?"

"I have no idea."

She contemplated him in silence.

"I know I should know more about the woman who is carrying my baby," he said apologetically and with disgust, too. "It isn't as if I didn't ask her questions and want to know more about her. She just wasn't forthcoming."

"She kept secrets."

The way Cassie stated it instead of asking it brought his worries to the forefront, too. He'd already realized he couldn't trust Eva, but he hadn't known whether to be afraid for her or angry at her.

"In some ways she was open," he said. She was a distraction when he'd needed it. Or so he'd thought. Turned out he was wrong, but that didn't relieve him of his responsibilities. "It was like she wanted to keep herself mysterious, like it would keep me more interested."

"Would it?"

He considered the possibility. "Maybe. To a point. Intrigue boosts adrenaline and interest, but it had gotten tired."

"Yeah. The rush is great—for a while. How about education?" Cassie asked.

"Currently attending business school. The firm was paying for a paralegal course. She was allowed to attend classes during work hours." He passed her a piece of paper. "Make and model of the car she drives, and the license plate."

"Outstanding. Who is her obstetrician?"

Heath handed her a second Rolodex card, which also listed the hospital where the baby was to be born.

"Did you take Lamaze classes? Do you plan on being there for the birth?"

"No and no."

"Did you go to her doctor's appointments with her?"

"No." He almost had, once, when she was to have an ultrasound. He changed his mind at his front door.

Cassie capped the pen and bounced it against her palm as she eyed him. "You said you don't get out much."

"Right."

"Do you get out at all, Mr. Raven?"

"Heath. And, no."

"For how long?"

"Three years."

He let her do the math. He hadn't stepped foot out of his house since his son died.

"You don't open the blinds, either."

"No."

She didn't ask why, but if she had, he wouldn't have answered. It wasn't any of her business.

"Okay," she said, slipping the pen into her notebook.

"I've got enough to get started, except I need a photo, if you've got one."

He handed her a file folder.

"Young," Cassie said when she saw the photo inside.

"Twenty-three. I'm thirty-nine. I figure you're wondering. Yeah, she was young." And they didn't have much in common. "There's a picture of the baby."

She turned the page. He'd made a copy of the ultrasound taken months ago.

She turned the picture sideways, then upside down. "I've never seen one of these before."

He outlined the body parts. "Head. Nose. Chin. Arms. Fingers. Legs."

Cassie smiled. "If you say so. Do you know the sex?"

He tapped the page. "Legs are crossed."

"Or there's nothing to see. Could be a little girl."

"Could be."

She closed her notebook. He handed her an envelope with a check for the retainer she'd told him on the phone that ARC would require. They walked downstairs in silence.

At the front door she stopped. "Are you in love with her?"

Like he believed in love anymore? "No."

"Yet you would've married her."

He'd already said as much. He felt no need to explain himself.

"There's something I need you to do," Cassie said, her tone businesslike but her eyes gentle. "The investigation may take a turn or reach a point where you will have to leave the house, maybe to go with me somewhere or even to go alone if Eva calls and needs you.

You need to get your mind in a place where you can do that."

"I already have." He would do anything for his child. Anything. Including fighting Eva for custody, something he wouldn't have done before. She obviously wasn't fit to be a mother. "What can I do in the meantime?"

"Let me get things rolling first. Sometimes these kinds of things solve themselves fairly fast. If you think of anything else that might be important, give me a call."

She held out her hand. He took it automatically, one businessperson to another, concluding a deal. He started to let go, but she tightened her hold.

He got caught in the unwavering intensity of her eyes.

"I will find your child," she said with conviction.

His throat closed. He barely stopped himself from yanking her into his arms in gratitude.

He believed her.

Two

It didn't take Cassie long at her computer that afternoon to come up with Eva's date of birth, social security number, current address and previous address. The rest would take more digging. She expected that the interview with the roommate, Darcy, would yield the most concrete information—unless Eva had been as secretive with Darcy as she'd been with Heath.

Cassie hit the print key then pushed away from her desk and stretched, loosening her shoulder muscles. While her documents and notes printed, she would call Eva's obstetrician. She picked up the phone, started to punch in the numbers, then stopped the call before it went through and dialed Heath instead.

"It's Cassie Miranda," she said when he answered.

"You have news?"

She heard expectation in his voice and was sorry not to be able to give him good news. She didn't know much about Eva yet, but Cassie knew this much—people who used children were the lowest form of humanity. "I'm sorry, no. I'm about to call her OB's office and pretend I'm her. Does she have an accent?"

A few beats passed. She figured he was dealing with the disappointment of no news. "No accent," he said finally.

"Any distinctive speech patterns? Does she say 'you know' a lot? Or 'like'? Anything like that?"

"She giggles."

Cassie cringed. "A lot?"

"Yes. Even more when she's nervous."

Great. "Can you give me an example?"

Silence, then, "Right. That's something I would do."

She smiled at his sarcasm. "I think I would've liked to hear you try." She looked at Eva's photo when he said nothing further, trying to picture the two of them together. They didn't fit. She was a girl-next-door type, with red hair and freckles, and he seemed worldly, even in his grief for the son he lost and the yet-to-be-born child now missing.

And he's a hermit, don't forget. Not exactly your ordinary sophisticate.

"Any other ideas come to you?" she asked.

"She likes to shop."

Cassie grinned. She was getting used to his interesting way of offering information, direct and vague at the same time. "Any place in particular?"

"She likes a bargain. Said she's never paid full price for anything and she never would."

"She likes a bargain as in thrift stores—or the semi-annual sale at Nordstrom?"

"Both, I would guess. And consignment shops. She'd found one that sold only maternity clothes."

"Can't be too many of those in the city." She grabbed her phone book from her credenza and placed it on her desktop. "Thanks. I'll check it out."

As soon as she hung up she called the doctor's office, knowing she was cutting it close to quitting time. She drummed her pen on the desk as the voice menu prompted her with choices to make, then she chose option three, which had to do with making appointments.

"Hi," she said when an actual human being came on the line. "This is Eva Brooks. I've done the *silliest* thing." That was as close to a giggle as she was going to get. "I lost the card showing my next appointment. Can you tell me when I'm supposed to come in, please?"

"Brooks, did you say?"

"Yes. Eva."

Cassie heard the distinctive sound of keystrokes on a keyboard.

"You're Dr. Sorenson's patient?"

"Yes." Did she sound cheerful enough? Innocent enough? *Please don't make me giggle.*

"Do you go by a different first name?"

Cassie knew she didn't have to pursue it. Another of Eva's deceits. Was she really even pregnant? Was it all a scheme to squeeze money out of Heath? Prey on his vulnerabilities?

"I'm sorry. Did you say Sorenson?" Cassie asked. "I wasn't paying attention. I dialed wrong. My mistake."

She dropped the receiver into the cradle and stared sightlessly at the phone.

"Cass?"

She roused herself as James Paladin rapped his knuckles on her desk. Like her, he'd been hired as an investigator nine months ago when the L.A.-based ARC Security & Investigations opened its branch office in San Francisco.

"You okay?" he asked.

"Yeah." She straightened, paid attention. "Yeah. You need something, Jamey?"

"To brainstorm the Kobieski case, if you've got time."

She looked at her watch—five o'clock exactly. She didn't want to tell Heath over the phone. He'd had enough heartache already. She could at least soften the blow in person. But the commute traffic from San Francisco across the bridge would be horrendous now. If she waited an hour or two...

"Sure," she said. "I've got time."

From a downstairs bedroom Heath watched Cassie walk from her car toward his house, her strides purposeful. She'd called a few minutes ago, as she was driving across the bridge, alerting him she was coming, an unnecessary thoughtfulness since he never went anywhere and she knew it.

What had she found out? Something important or she would've told him over the phone. Something good, he hoped.

He tried to turn off his appreciation of her as a woman, but he couldn't. She was beautiful, pure and simple. And unaware of it. If she used makeup at all, it was minimal.

She pulled her hair back into a simple braid. No fuss, no muss. Her body was athletic and curvy, a one-two punch to a man who'd recently convinced himself that celibacy should be the only path for him from now on, but who obviously wasn't capable of such a sacrifice.

Aside from her spectacular face and body she had a mind that appealed, too. And she didn't giggle.

The doorbell rang. He hadn't meant to make her wait, but he'd been distracted by thoughts of her—didn't want to be, but he was. This time, however, he would control his response, even though her passion-filled promise that she would find his baby was as seductive as her physical being.

He set the little white teddy bear he'd been holding onto a nearby rocking chair and headed into the foyer. He opened the door, hope in his heart.

All hope fled when he looked in her eyes. "Tell me," he said.

"Can we sit?" she asked.

"Tell me."

Her mouth tightened. "Are you sure she's pregnant?"

Not dead. Not dead, or she would've said so right away. Relief rushed through him like three straight shots of bourbon, hot and dizzying. "Yes."

"Positive?"

"Why?"

"Because Dr. Sorenson's office says she wasn't a patient. How do you know for sure she was pregnant?"

"I felt the baby move."

"I don't mean to question you on this, but—"

"She let me put my hand on her abdomen many times while she visited. Sometimes she lifted her blouse enough that I could watch the baby move inside her. I've been through a pregnancy before, Cassie."

She propped her fists on her hips and looked at the floor, blowing out a breath. "I thought she'd been toying with you. Playing you for—" She stopped.

"A fool? A sucker?" he finished.

She shook her head. "A decent, but vulnerable man. One with money."

He let the words linger for a few seconds.

"What's the next step?" he asked, ignoring the implications of what she'd said. "You can't call every doctor in the city."

"Yes, I can."

It took him a moment to let that idea sink in. "You're kidding."

"I'll start with the obstetricians, of course."

"You can't possibly—"

"Yes. I can. And I'll try to hook up with the roommate tomorrow. I think that's our best chance for information. The problem I'm going to have with calling the doctors is that there are so many group practices. I would be asked which doctor, and I can't name more than one."

"So, it's a long shot."

She smiled at the understatement. "We could get lucky."

He admired her resolve. "What can I do?"

"Be here if she calls or comes by."

"That goes without saying."

She studied him. "Are you sure you'll be able to leave the house if you need to?"

He didn't like being questioned, wasn't used to it. "Has it occurred to you that I choose to stay in my house? That it's a conscious choice I made?" He leaned toward her. "I will do what needs to be done."

"Why haven't—"

"The subject's not on the table, Cassie."

It ended not only that particular discussion about why he didn't leave the house but also their conversation in general. He walked her to the front door.

"Did you design this house?" she asked.

"I did."

"It's spectacular."

"But?"

"No but."

"Yes, there is." He heard it in her voice even if she didn't realize it.

She shook her head.

Ah. Keeps her own counsel. He liked that.

"If Eva had simply disappeared, without leaving a note," Cassie said, her hand on the doorknob, "this whole situation would be different. The police would get involved. We would have access to their resources. I still think someone at her office could help."

"I refuse to cause problems for her at work if she's just having some kind of hormone overload. I'm already disregarding her wishes by hiring you to try to find her, for which I feel no guilt whatsoever, by the way. That's *my* child she's got. *My* life she's playing with, as well." He shoved his hands through his hair, locked his fingers behind his neck and made himself calm down. "Look, I'm trying to do the right thing here. It's my fault she's pregnant."

"You know, Heath, these days I think we consider pregnancy a dual responsibility."

"She was young."

"Not that young. And you were vulnerable."

It was the second time she'd used that word to describe him. He didn't like it. Who was she to come to that conclusion so quickly?

"Vulnerable doesn't mean weak," she said, somehow reading his mind. "It means you'd been hurt so deeply you didn't want to survive, but you did, so you have to deal with it, but it's harder for you than for others. Most people can't cope too long without the company of other people, of a compatible partner, no matter how short-lived."

"Personal experience?"

"I haven't lost a child." She opened the door. "I'll be in touch when I have news."

"I want progress reports, not just news."

"No problem."

He didn't want her to leave…but he couldn't ask her to stay.

Three

Cassie grabbed an official-looking envelope from the passenger seat then headed into Eva's apartment building. The hallway was surprisingly bright and cheerful. Someone was playing a clarinet, repeating the same section again and again. The fragrance of sautéing onions drifted, mingling with something spicy. Curry? It was five o'clock on Friday night. She hoped to catch Eva's roommate before she headed out for the evening.

Eva and Darcy lived on the third floor. Cassie climbed the stairs then knocked on the door. After fifteen seconds she tried again. No one answered. No sounds came from inside.

She propped her shoulders against the wall next to the door to wait. So much of her job involved patience. She surprised even herself that she not only coped well with all the waiting involved but that she didn't even mind it most of the time. Surveillance was often boring, but she was so grateful to be working for ARC that she didn't even mind the long, dull hours sitting in her car waiting and watching for something to happen. Her life had changed drastically since Quinn had hired her late last year.

An image of Heath popped into her head. A fascinating man, simmering with emotion he carefully controlled. Talented and intelligent. Angry. Somber.

He had good reasons to be somber. Cassie had learned that his five-year-old son, Kyle, had died in a school bus accident three years ago, and that Heath had been with him but couldn't save him. Heath was still married at the time, so the divorce had obviously come after they lost their son.

The death of a child, a divorce and now the disappearance of the woman carrying his baby—Cassie was surprised he was speaking in complete sentences.

She thought back to the look on his face when he'd opened the door to her last night. The hope that died fast when she didn't have good news for him. She'd wanted to put her arms around him and tell him it was going to be okay. His pain sent her reeling back to her own, different but still caused by other people taking away control, making you—

Someone was jogging up the stairs. Cassie pushed herself away from the wall just as a woman in her early twenties rounded the corner. Her hair was black and chin-length, a choppy cut popular with her age group. Her gold nose stud reflected light from a wall sconce. She wore a ruffled minidress over form-fitting jeans, a look that worked for her.

She challenged Cassie with her eyes.

"Are you Darcy?" Cassie asked.

"Why?"

"I'm looking for Eva Brooks."

She slid her key into the lock. "Get in line."

"I'm sorry?"

"Eva bailed a month ago." The door opened. "I had to take a second job so I could cover the rent." She looked Cassie up and down. "What d'you want with her?"

A month ago? "I have a document for her."

Darcy eyed the envelope Cassie held. "What kinda document?"

"I really can't say."

"Well, I can't help you."

She started to shut the door. Cassie put her hand out to stop it from closing. "I really need to find her. It might mean a lot of money for her, if she's the right Eva Brooks." It was the right tactic. At the word *money* Darcy paid attention.

"She owes me rent and stuff," Darcy said.

Cassie waited.

"Look," the young woman said, "I don't know where she's at. The lawyer she works for called, too, but I couldn't help him, either."

"How long have you been roommates?"

"Couple of years. She got herself knocked up, though, so I was kinda glad she left 'cuz I really didn't want a baby around, you know?"

"I'm sure. Did she talk about the father? Maybe she's with him."

She snorted. "I don't think so."

"Why not?"

"Too old. Too stodgy. I don't know. She had a list of reasons why she wasn't hanging out with him."

Cassie could see how Eva would perceive Heath as stodgy, especially if she didn't see past his pain. But, old? "Still, she is pregnant," she said to Darcy. "It would make sense that she would turn to him."

"Maybe. Her mail's still coming here, though. Bills. I'm not paying 'em."

"Could I take a look?"

Darcy frowned. "Who *are* you?"

Cassie gave her a business card.

"A P.I.?" She gave a low whistle. "Sweet."

"Yeah, it is."

"She got a rich old uncle who died and left her money?"

"Something like that. Maybe I can track her down through her mail, then you can get the money she owes you."

Darcy hesitated. For a second Cassie thought she'd convinced her, then Darcy shook her head. "It wouldn't be right. And I really gotta go. If I'm late even a minute, they dock an hour's pay."

"I wouldn't open the mail. Just see who sent it."

"Naw."

"You've got my number," Cassie said as the door closed.

She made her way to her car. Now what?

She didn't like how this case was stacking up. Eva had lied more than once and now had left no trail. It was rare that someone could just disappear, but especially someone eight months pregnant.

Cassie decided there were no leads to follow, no more calls that could be made at the moment. She could give Heath an update by phone then go back to the office and do the paperwork she'd ignored on her two other cases. Or she could call a friend and go out to dinner, maybe dancing. Blow off a little steam. Find a reason to laugh.

She pulled her cell phone from her jacket pocket. After a minute she put it away. She didn't know why she tried to pretend with herself. She wanted to see him in person. It was stupid. She didn't get mixed up with clients, and she especially shouldn't get mixed up with this one, who had twice as much baggage as she did—and that was a lot, although hers had been stored in an overhead bin for a long time.

She should do them both a favor and just call him and let him know how it went with Darcy.

Then she pictured the look in his eyes when he'd said his child was missing.

She glanced at her watch. The traffic would be miserable.

She gripped the steering wheel. There was nothing to accomplish by going to his house. She would only add to an attraction that should be buried in business-like behavior.

If only someone had cared about me like he cares for his unborn child.

Cassie blew out a long breath. Okay, so she was drawn to the wounded man in more ways than were good for her. Decency was a big lure. She'd known too many not-so-decent people.

She leaned her forehead against the steering wheel.

He had to be especially lonely now. The hours must drag by as he waited for word.

She resigned herself to the inevitable, started her car then eased into traffic.

Heath eyed the telephone on the desk beside him. If Cassie had news she would call. He knew that. But the waiting was almost too much to handle. She'd called once today to say she had nothing to report. That was hours ago.

He shoved away from his desk. He couldn't work.

After Kyle died Heath had thrown himself into work, resting only when he fell asleep at the computer. Mary Ann had left him the day of the funeral. It should have been the least creative, least productive time of his career. Instead he'd overflowed with ideas. He'd designed buildings that would never be built, futuristic-looking skyscrapers beyond man's ability to engineer. But he'd also produced winning, workable designs—buildings he'd never seen except in video, whether already constructed or under construction now.

A psychologist would undoubtedly tell him it was avoidance, that he was only delaying his grief by immersing himself in work. And to a psychologist, that might be the easy truth. Heath knew it was much more complicated.

When Eva told him she was pregnant he was stunned at first, then in denial. But he'd come to believe that the child would be his chance to do it over, and do it right.

The doorbell rang. He dragged himself out of his office, grabbing his wallet as he went. He'd ordered dinner from Villa Romano.

It wasn't the delivery boy at the door, however.

"Am I interrupting you?" Cassie asked.

Except for the fact she was wearing a blue shirt instead of white, she was dressed as she had been yesterday. Her uniform, he decided. Damn but it looked good on her. He tried to read her expression. *Do you have good news for me or bad?*

He fought the urge to take her in his arms. His need for human touch—her touch—came from out of the blue.

"I'm sorry," she said, angling as if to leave. "I should've called."

He'd stared at her in silence for too long. She didn't know he was fighting a rush of feeling for her—the last thing he needed right then. Especially since he couldn't define what that feeling was.

"No. Cassie, I'm glad to see you."

A refurbished postal Jeep left dust in its wake as it sped up the driveway and came to a quick stop.

"Dinner," Heath told Cassie.

"Hey," said a kid with sixteen or so piercings and tattoos down his arms. He hopped onto the porch. "How's it goin'?"

Heath traded the boy money for the take-out containers. "Thanks."

He jogged off with a backward wave.

Heath moved aside to let Cassie in.

"I was presumptuous," she said.

"Not at all." He waited for her to say something about Eva. Anything.

"I don't have any news to speak of," she said, following him into the kitchen. "I made a lot of calls to obstetricians' offices, without results."

He wondered how many more blows he would have to take. *Damn you, Eva.* "Would you like a beer or something?"

"No, thanks." She leaned against the counter. "I went to her previous apartment, but I didn't find anyone at home who remembered her. I'll go back tomorrow when I might catch a few more tenants. Of course people are often out running errands on Saturday, but it's worth a shot."

"Okay."

"I contacted her business school, but they're on a two-week break before the next semester. They wouldn't tell me if she was registered. Then I went to the two maternity-wear consignment shops. One of the clerks recognized her photo but said she hadn't been in for a couple of months. Which makes sense. At some point, you've got enough maternity clothes. Anyway, I left her my card and asked her to call if Eva came back."

"You were busy."

"Yeah. And just before I came here, I met Darcy. Eva left the apartment a month ago, no notice. Darcy doesn't know where she went, and she's pretty ticked off that she's been left with the full rent to pay."

"Too ticked off to give you any information?"

"I'm pretty sure she doesn't know anything, but I'll try her again, too. She may know more than she thinks."

He opened a bottle of beer for himself. If Darcy didn't have any information, what chance did they have? Eva could be anywhere. With anyone. He may never see his baby. Ever.

What the hell had he done to deserve this? Hadn't he

paid a big enough price already? He took a long swig of beer then plunked the bottle on the counter.

Cassie rested her hand on his. "We'll find them. We will."

He didn't pull his hand away, but he tried to figure her out. "You could've called and told me this, Cassie."

She straightened, probably because he'd sounded accusatory. "I could have."

Why didn't you? "I've got enough ravioli for two," he said by way of invitation, testing the waters.

She hesitated. They seemed to do that a lot with each other.

"I appreciate the offer," she said, "but I need to get going."

He'd read her wrong. It only served to frustrate him more. "Just thought I'd ask."

"Thanks." She walked out of the kitchen.

He followed. His mood, not good to start with, got blacker. Just yesterday he'd been glad she was the investigator on his case. Now he wasn't sure.

"I don't know how much I can do until Monday and the doctors' offices are open again. I contacted every local hospital and will continue to do so," she said.

She'd been as efficient as he'd expected. But he still didn't know why she'd come instead of called, especially since she wouldn't even share dinner with him.

She waited, apparently giving him the opportunity to say something. When he didn't, she opened the door and stepped outside. It was a beautiful evening, warm and breezy, a good night for driving the silver convertible parked in his garage. The one he hadn't driven in three years. The one that undoubtedly wouldn't start. He should take care of that.

"I'm sorry," Cassie said, then walked away.

"For what?"

"For disturbing your evening."

He didn't tell her she was wrong, because she *had* disturbed his evening—and he liked the disturbance. But it was better that she leave.

He watched her walk away, her pace even quicker than usual. He'd never been drawn to a woman this fast before. He'd known Mary Ann for months before they dated. Eva hadn't been any temptation at all until almost a year of seeing her once a week and then only because of her overt come-on. But Cassie—

She was gone. He returned to the house to wait for the phone to ring. He ate dinner because he knew he needed fuel, then he retreated to his office. Midnight came. One o'clock. Two. He fought sleep. Until recently every time he slept he heard Kyle call for him. *Daddy. Dad-dy!* He woke up sweating and trying to catch his breath. Recently he'd been hearing a baby cry.

He jerked up, hitting his head on his work lamp. The baby was crying again—

No. It was his doorbell. He blinked to clear his eyes and looked at the clock. Four thirty-five. He'd fallen asleep at his worktable.

The bell rang again. He shook his head and hurried out of the room, down the stairs. He glanced out the glass panel next to the door.

Eva. Holding a baby.

Four

Heath yanked open the door. His gaze went to the bundle in Eva's arms then to her face. Her eyes were blank, her hair straggly, her freckles prominent.

"Come in," he urged her, picking up the diaper bag she'd set on the ground beside her. He looked over her shoulder and spotted her car. He hadn't heard her drive up, he'd been so soundly asleep.

He guided her toward the living room. She sat down gingerly. He took a seat beside her and waited, knowing he couldn't push her for information but wanting to yell at her, *Where have you been? Why did you worry me like that?*

"It's a boy," she said.

A tornado of emotion spun through him, fast and furious, destroying the walls of resistance built months ago, obliterating uncertainty in one gigantic whirl. A boy. A son.

"Do you want to hold him?" Eva asked solemnly.

"Yes." He rubbed his hands on his thighs then reached for the baby. The blanket fell away from his face and Heath looked at his son for the first time. He wriggled, pursed his lips and arched his back but didn't open his eyes. He had dark hair, a sweet pink face. Heath's eyes blurred as he dragged a finger lightly down his son's face. "He's perfect." He reached to take Eva's hand. "Thank you."

She stared at him for a long time, then she lifted her chin. "Do you want him?"

"Of course I want him. I've told you so all along."

"I mean—" she pulled her hand free "—do you want to keep him yourself? Forever?"

His heart slammed against his sternum. "What?"

"If you do, I'll leave him here with you."

"Why?"

"Do you or don't you?"

Heath tried to make sense of what she was doing. Why would she offer such a thing? Postpartum depression? If so, undoubtedly she would be back to claim her child.

But in the meantime, no one else would have his son. "I do," he said simply.

"How much is he worth to you?"

Shock ripped through Heath. She was selling him? He didn't know her at all. He realized he *never* knew her.

My son is worth everything. How could he place a dollar value on his own child? "I can write you a check for ten thousand right now. If you want more, you'll have to wait until the bank opens on Monday."

"I'll take it."

He hesitated. So little? She knew he could afford much more than that.

Something wasn't right. But when he looked at his son, the thought fled. "Will you sign a letter agreeing to my assuming full legal custody of him?"

"Sure, why not?"

He started to put his son in Eva's arms while he tended to business but realized he couldn't let go of him. "Come up to my office. We'll draft an agreement."

He dictated the note as she typed it, her hands shaking, then they both signed it. He wrote out the check and gave it to her.

"You'd better not stop payment on this or I'll take him back," she said coldly. "I only have to claim severe postpartum depression. Everyone will understand that."

He was more concerned that the document wouldn't hold up in court. "Did you give him a name?"

"No."

"When was he born?"

"Yesterday."

"Yesterday? Shouldn't he still be in the hospital?"

"No." She started to leave the room, her face ashen, legs wobbly.

"Eva," he said, touching her shoulder. "You need to rest. Stay here. Sleep for a while. Have something to eat."

"I can't." Her eyes shifted to the baby, then she ducked her head and hurried out of the office and down the stairs. She flung open the front door and raced out.

"Wait!" he called, but she didn't stop. He tucked the

blanket more tightly around his son and followed her into the yard. "Where can I contact you?"

"There's a bottle in the diaper bag. You just have to warm it." She got in her car and slammed the door, then she was gone.

He stood there until he could no longer hear her engine, then he walked back into the house. The baby made a noise. Heath pulled the blanket from his face and stood in the foyer staring at him. His son. His second chance.

He leaned over and kissed his tiny forehead. He felt dizzy, almost nauseated. He made his way into the living room and sat down to stare at the boy. Soon he started to fuss, then whimper, then cry. Heath dug through the diaper bag in search of a bottle.

He cried in earnest now. Heath didn't know whether to heat the tiny bottle in the microwave or—

He decided to run hot water into a bowl. It might take longer but it couldn't melt the nipple or anything.

While he waited for the bottle to warm, he walked the kitchen floor, whispering soothing words, holding his son close, bouncing him lightly. His cries got louder. Heath tested the milk. Not warm yet. He ran more hot water, then picked up the telephone. He glanced at the business card sitting on his kitchen counter.

Five-fifteen in the morning, he noticed as the phone was ringing. Would she mind?

"Hello?" she said, her voice layered with sleep, but trying not to show it.

"Cassie?" he said above the baby's cries.

"Heath? Is that—?"

"It's my son. Can you come over?"

* * *

Cassie waited anxiously at Heath's front door. The usual silence surrounded the house. No sound of a baby crying. No birds singing in the early dawn.

She prepared herself for meeting Eva, for being polite to the woman who'd caused Heath grief and worry on top of what he already lived with.

She prepared herself, too, for the fact she wouldn't see him after this. The issue was closed. She hadn't even had a chance to find the baby herself, to solve the case, to show him, frankly, how good she was at her job. She should be glad it was over. She *was* glad it was over, for Heath's sake, but he would be completely involved in his new life now.

Maybe Eva would even agree to marry him, and they could live together as a family. The baby deserved that opportunity. Eva should give it a chance.

The front door opened. His arms were empty. He should be smiling. He wasn't smiling.

"Thank you for coming," he said, gesturing her in.

Cassie stepped across the threshold and into the foyer. The lights were on in the living room but Cassie saw no signs of the redheaded Eva.

"Where's the baby?"

"Asleep. In his basket."

He led her toward the living room. She spotted a wicker bassinet on the coffee table.

"And Eva?"

"Gone."

"Where?"

"I don't know."

Cassie bent over the bassinet, saw that it was lined

with yellow gingham. "You don't— Oh! Oh, how sweet." He was wrapped in a blue blanket, his tiny face barely visible. Her heart melted. She'd felt a bond with him from the moment she knew of his existence, her concern for his welfare her priority. Seeing him in person cemented everything.

She straightened. "What do you mean you don't know where she is?"

"She sold him to me for ten thousand dollars, then she left."

It took her a second to comprehend what he'd just told her. "Seriously?"

"Signed, sealed and delivered."

She sat on the sofa but kept her hand on the basket as Heath related what happened.

"What do you think?" she asked. "It sounds like she was emotional."

"Definitely. But there are all kinds of emotions, Cassie. I can't pretend to know what she was feeling. I only know the truth of what's here in front of me—my son. He needs me to take care of him now, no matter what happens in the future."

She looked into the bassinet as the baby stirred. "Yes. First things first."

"I doubt the paper she signed will hold up in court."

"I doubt it, too. But it's a start. You need to have him checked by a pediatrician. You need his birth certificate as soon as it's available. And he needs a name." The baby's eyes opened. Cassie smiled at him. "You need a name, don't you, sweet pea?"

Heath lifted the baby out of the basket. "Daniel. Daniel Patrick."

"That's nice. Is there some significance?"

"My father's name—before he turned hippie and started calling himself Journey."

"You're the product of hippies?" Cassie laughed.

He didn't react, just stared at her for a few seconds, but she couldn't figure out why.

"It's the truth," he said finally. "My mother calls herself Crystal. They live on a commune in New Hampshire."

"Did you grow up there?"

"Yeah. I couldn't wait to go away to college."

There was fondness in his voice, though, indicating he might have resented his upbringing then but not now.

"They're into macrobiotic diets," he added.

"That's grains and vegetables, isn't it?"

"It's cardboard."

She smiled. "I like steak."

"Me, too. And ordering in."

Daniel started to fuss. Cassie clenched her hands. She wanted to hold him, but Heath hadn't offered, so she leaned close and sang. "The itsy bitsy spider—"

"Don't."

Startled at his vehement tone, Cassie sat back. The baby wailed. "Don't what?"

"Sing." He bounced Daniel.

"Why not? Babies love singing. It calms them."

"I don't have to explain myself." He tried to shush the baby, who had worked up a full head of steam.

Cassie wondered about Heath's sanity. Or was he just stressed over everything that had just happened? "Maybe he's hungry," she offered.

"He had a bottle right before you got here."

"Maybe he needs a diaper change. Do you want me

to check?" When he didn't answer, she looked straight at him. He's afraid to trust me, she realized. He's probably afraid to trust anyone. "I'll take good care of him," she said gently.

He stared at her for at least ten seconds. "Yeah. Okay."

The exchange was a little awkward, but soon Daniel was settled in her arms like he belonged there.

Like he belonged there.

Cassie didn't question the feeling. She blinked back tears as love for this total stranger flooded her. This helpless little boy whose mother abandoned him and whose father wanted to do the right thing, but who needed to open up his heart and soul again. Learn to laugh and live life. Go back into the world. Daniel should not grow up a hermit, just because his father chose to be one.

"Do you have diapers?" she asked.

"In the nursery. Follow me." He led her across the foyer into a yellow bedroom so bright and sunny that it seemed like something out of a fantasy, not a room in this gloomy house.

"This is nice," she said. "Did Eva help you put the room together?"

"No. I wanted it to be a surprise."

She set Daniel on the changing table. Careful not to disturb his cord she changed a very wet diaper for a dry one, then wrapped him up again. Still he fussed. She tucked him against her chest and swung back and forth. His cries grew quieter, then they stopped. He'd fallen asleep.

Heath had hovered over them like the protective father he was. "Where'd you learn about taking care of babies?"

"Here and there."

"Baby-sitting?"

"In a manner of speaking. I spent a lot of time in foster homes. There were always babies to be tended."

She felt his gaze intensify but ignored it. She'd never wanted sympathy for what she'd gone through. It was done. She'd moved on. So instead she sat in the rocking chair, satisfying her need to hold Daniel while also keeping him asleep with the motion. She looked around the room. "Do you have everything he needs?"

"Except formula. Eva brought ten bottles altogether, so I'm okay until the stores open. I'll have someone deliver it."

He'd gotten too used to doing that, she realized. Letting the world come to him. It wasn't a good example for his son.

Plus he wouldn't let her sing to him.

"I need to hire a nanny," he said, crouching in front of her.

"I imagine you do."

"I could use your help finding one."

"Me?" What did she know about hiring a nanny? "There are agencies for that. I can do background checks on the candidates, if you want, additional to the ones the agency does."

"That would be great." He rested a hand on Daniel's tiny body. "In the meantime, though, would you stay here and help me with him?"

"You know how to take care of a baby."

He met her gaze. "I know he needs to be fed and changed and bathed. I've already fed him one bottle, but there's more to baby care than heating up some formula and popping a bottle in his mouth."

She looked into Daniel's innocent face. She would move heaven and earth for him. She wanted a home where he would thrive not just survive. She wanted to see that he got one, but she already had a dangerous and foolish attraction to Heath, and he had more problems than she wanted to take on.

And then there was the other issue, the big one—there was no way she could spend the night. He would know....

"I can't," she said. "I'm sorry. I just can't."

Five

A little while later, Cassie glanced at her watch as she unlocked her office door and stepped inside. Only ten o'clock. It seemed like hours later. She was still shaking from leaving Heath like that. Leaving Daniel. She'd wanted to stay. She couldn't stay. She'd never been so torn.

"Jamey?" she called. His car was parked outside.

"In my office," he shouted.

She wandered down the hall and propped a shoulder against James Paladin's doorjamb. He wore khakis and a plaid shirt, the sleeves rolled up a few turns. His dark brown hair looked wet from a shower, his eyes friendly and inquisitive. "Here we are on another Saturday morning. No rest for the weary," he said with a half smile and gesturing to the pile of paperwork on his desktop. "Did you know when you took this job you would never get a day off?"

"Did you ever have a day off when you were a bounty hunter?" she parried.

"Touché. Anyway, thanks for coming in so quickly."

She took a seat opposite his desk. "No problem. I was out and about anyway. Why'd you call? What's going on?"

"I got a call from Sam Remington."

Sam was one of the big bosses, one of the three original owners of ARC Security & Investigations. He worked out of the Los Angeles branch. The fourth owner, Quinn Gerard, was her immediate supervisor, but Quinn was on a case out of town. "New case?" she asked.

"Sort of. For you, though, not me."

"Why didn't Sam call me directly?"

"He did. He said your phone was turned off."

Oh. Right. She'd turned it off until she got back into the city, figuring she would check messages later, not wanting to talk to Heath. Jamey had called the minute she'd turned it back on and asked her to meet him at the office.

"Anyway, here's the deal," he said. "Sam's wife—"

"The good Senator Dana Sterling."

"Yeah, well, Dana is friends with your newest client, Heath Raven."

"Really?" She wondered how that happened? Obviously before he imprisoned himself. It struck her then what was going on. "No." She sprang out of her chair, shook her head several times. "I am not playing nanny for Mr. Raven."

"Apparently you are. Orders from the boss."

"He went over my head," she said in disbelief. "I told him no and he went over my head. That…that—" She couldn't come up with a word to finish her thought. How dare he put her on the spot like that?

Okay. He wants to be play hard ball, she'll play with him. She would protect his baby, protect him from a mother cruel enough to run away, leaving the father wondering and waiting for days and then abandoning them both, but she also would cushion Daniel from a father who didn't have any joy to give to a child. Cassie had lived without joy. She would make sure Daniel didn't, at least for as long as she was living in that house.

Jamey leaned forward. "I've seen that look before, Cass."

"What look is that?" She stuffed her hands in her pockets, avoiding making eye contact.

"Mutinous. He's the client. He's paying the bill. You need to rein in."

"I'll do what I'm expected to do. He won't have any complaints about that. Someone needs to protect that baby."

He came up beside her. "Be careful, Cass. You can't save the whole world."

"What does that mean?"

"You're a crusader, and sometimes that's a good thing. But you could end up hurt if you don't win this battle."

"You're an expert on me now?"

"Yeah. I think I am. Something wrong with that?"

They stood almost toe to toe. It wasn't a confrontational moment but a revealing one. Cassie knew her own strengths and weaknesses, her own virtues and flaws.

"No," she said at last. "One of these days we'll have a little chat about you. I've got you pegged, too."

He laughed. "I'm sure you have. Listen, give me a call if there's anything I can do. Or if you need a shoulder to cry on. Or if Mr. Raven needs medical attention."

She punched him lightly on the shoulder, grinned, then grabbed her briefcase. He laid a hand on her arm as she started to walk past him.

"Some people can't be saved, Cass," he said, more serious than he'd been until then.

His words sent a chill through her. He'd seen too deeply into her. She was already a little obsessed with Heath, which was why she'd made herself leave. She recognized the signs, even though she'd never felt that way before, although maybe some of her obsession was that Heath came with a baby, a big lure for her.

"Keep in touch," he said.

"I will."

She felt his gaze on her, his concern, as she left the office. He and Quinn were like brothers to her instead of co-worker and boss.

But brothers were often overprotective for little reason, too. Not that she'd had any experience with brothers, but she'd heard it was true. Still, it was nice having people looking out for her.

Heath yanked open the front door for Cassie as she reached it.

"You pulled rank," she all but yelled at him over Daniel's wails. "You pulled rank!"

"I'm taking care of my son best way I know how." Damn but she was glorious. Color in her face, fire in her eyes. She'd laughed earlier when he'd told her about his hippie parents, and he'd been startled by how the sound had affected him, lightening his dark world. But this Cassie, this furious Cassie, turned him on.

"I didn't know hermits enjoyed such lofty company," she said, her eyes going to Danny constantly. He knew she wanted to hold him, to soothe his crying. "Senator Sterling is a friend of yours?"

"She and I go way back. And I'll use whatever contacts I need to if it helps my son."

"You act like I'm a miracle worker— How long has he been crying like that?" she asked, exasperated.

He had her. "An hour. He doesn't want a bottle."

"Did you buy pacifiers?" She reached for the baby. He gave him up much more willingly than the other time. He couldn't take another minute of the noise.

"No."

"We need some. You can get the stuff out of my car. Please." She tossed him her keys.

He decided the *please* was an afterthought to him as a client, not a man. He didn't want to be treated as a client. The natural Cassie brought life into his house. The investigator Cassie would be too cool, too competent.

"I doubt I can do anything different with Daniel, but I can give you a break, anyway," she said grudgingly.

He relaxed. Just having her there made a difference.

He folded his fingers around her keys. Get her stuff. To do that he would have to walk across the yard to the oak tree where her car was parked in the shade. He looked at the car, then at Cassie. He'd told her it was his choice to stay inside his house and that was true, but he'd gotten used to it, too.

"Lock it when you're done, okay?" Then she walked into the house, leaving him on his own.

Don't think about it. Just do it. Just do it.

Heath walked away then out the front door, not slowing for a second. He never took his eyes off her car. It was there, at the end of a long tunnel. *Focus. Focus. Keep your eyes on the car, on the goal. One step at a time. One victory at a time.*

He tried to judge whether he could carry everything in one trip and decided he could. He hefted the briefcase, suitcase and garment bag, locked the car, then walked steadily but quickly back to the house, shut the door with his foot and resisted leaning against it. He just kept moving, up the stairs, down the hall, into the guest room. He dropped her suitcase on the bed and hung the garment bag in the closet, then he checked the adjoining bathroom. Towels, washcloth, soap, shampoo. Okay. She probably brought everything else she needed.

He hurried downstairs. She hadn't emerged from Daniel's room by the time he was done. The quiet opened up his mind again. No more distractions, just the realization of what he'd accomplished. He'd gone beyond the porch. He'd walked a hundred feet. And he was still breathing, although his skin was damp and his mouth dry.

Too early for a bourbon and water? he wondered. Yeah. Way too early.

He went to the nursery instead and stepped quietly in. The rocking chair moved rhythmically.

Peace came over Heath in a rush, a soft place to land after so many years of chaos. He made himself inhale the feeling the way a woman put her face into a bouquet of roses, savoring, committing it to memory. He brushed his hand over his son's head, over the downy hair, the baby-warm skin. Daniel's dark blue eyes shifted sightlessly toward Heath. He sucked on Cassie's little finger like a pacifier.

She'd gotten him to stop crying almost instantly, he realized. He'd been too intent on going to the car to pay complete attention, but now he realized it hadn't taken her more than a minute to calm Daniel.

Cassie looked directly into Heath's eyes; her mouth widened into a leisurely smile—or was it a triumphant one? Damn but she would be nice to wake up with in the morning, all warm and sleepy, stretching her body under the sheet until it pulled away from her naked—

"Are you mad?" she asked, adjusting Daniel, sitting up a little more.

What kind of look had he had on his face? He'd wanted to kiss her, but to her he'd looked mad? Just as well, he decided. It was a complication they didn't need. "I'm not mad. Why would you think that?"

"You looked…I don't know. You looked upset."

"No." He held out his hands to take his son. "Thank you for quieting him."

"My pleasure." She stretched, just like he'd imagined she would, her long body arching, her nipples pressing against the fabric covering them.

A smart man—a man who learned from lessons gone wrong—wouldn't notice such things, but he apparently hadn't learned his lesson. He ached to take her breasts in his hands, to feel the hardness of her nipples and the softness of her flesh, to bury his face against her skin.

"Are you okay?" she asked, standing, crossing her arms as if she knew his thoughts. Her whole mood had changed. She didn't seem angry anymore. Maybe calming Daniel had done the same thing for her.

"I'm fine."

"You got everything from my car?"

He nodded.

"How'd it feel?"

"Like you brought enough to stay a week."

"I mean—" She stopped. "Another topic that's off-limits. Okay."

"The pediatrician was here while you were gone," he said, changing the subject altogether. "He said Daniel is in fine shape."

"Must be nice to have your kind of connections. I don't know any doctors who make house calls these days."

"We've been friends for years." Jake Mercer had been Kyle's pediatrician, too. Heath had designed a house for Jake and his wife. Although Heath was known principally for his skyscrapers, he occasionally designed a house for someone special. "He wants to see Daniel in a week. Sooner if we have any problems."

"Will you try to go to his office?"

"That's my plan." They walked out of the room together but stopped outside the door and looked at each other.

"Where are we headed?" she asked.

"Damned if I know."

"Well, maybe I should unpack."

"Your room is upstairs, second door on the right." *Across from mine.*

She started up the stairs, but stopped. "I apologize for losing my temper."

"No need to apologize. It was an honest reaction. I like honesty."

"I felt like a kid on my first job, having the boss order me like that."

"I'm sorry. I didn't know any other way to get you back here. I need you."

Her entire demeanor changed. Magic words, apparently. It was only the truth.

"I'll unpack. Do we have groceries or should I go get some? I could fix steaks for dinner."

Except for when his parents visited, no one ever made him dinner. He had guests over now and then, but he ordered in or sometimes they brought food. But having someone else in his kitchen, sharing the space, cleaning up together—it had been so long. "I've got steaks in the freezer. I called my parents to tell them the news," he added as she reached the top of the stairs. "I expect they'll be out to visit at some point."

"Maybe they could stay for a while, and you wouldn't need a nanny."

"I don't plan to make them that comfortable."

Cassie laughed as she walked away. The sound echoed in his big, empty house, filling it, lightening the gloom again. He looked at Daniel, who was still asleep in his arms. "I'm going to have to be very careful," he whispered to his son. "She could be a hard habit to break. Have to be careful for her sake, too, don't you think? Or is that egotistical?" Was it? He thought he saw mutual interest, but maybe not. He had no doubt that Daniel was the draw for her, but maybe him, too, a little?

He resisted the temptation to follow her up the stairs, to talk to her while she put things away. He wondered about her life in foster care. Why had she been put there? Was the experience good or bad? Why had she chosen to become a private investigator? Was it tied to her past somehow?

Would she even answer those kinds of questions? He'd hired her to do a job. Anything beyond that—like fixing dinner, which he'd never expected her to do—was a bonus. He shouldn't do anything to risk her quitting before he got some of the legal issues dealt with and a nanny in place. If she got mad enough, she would find a way to quit, no matter what her boss said.

A nanny. He didn't want someone else living full-time in his house with him, but could he manage having only daytime help? Would Daniel be the kind of baby to sleep most of the night or be up?

It was something Heath needed to know before he hired someone, or even started interviewing. That could take a few days, at least.

Sounds like a stall.

And your point is?

He cut off his internal dialogue then realized he hadn't moved since Cassie had jogged up the stairs. He should do something. If he put Daniel in his crib would he wake up? It was probably time for him to eat, anyway.

He paced. After a while he stopped at the bottom of the staircase. She'd had plenty of time to put her things away, so what was she doing?

He climbed the stairs and made his way down the hall. She'd left the door open. He should've announced his presence, he supposed, but he didn't want to startle Daniel.

He peeked into the room. She was standing at the window, the blinds not only open but raised, leaving a clear view of his property, overgrown and wild. He hadn't seen it from the upstairs angle for—well, for too long.

"Did you want something?" she asked, not turning around.

He'd wondered if she knew he was there. "Just checking that everything is okay with your room."

She faced him. "It's great."

"I'm across the hall."

"Okay." She walked toward him, her gaze on him until she got close, then dropping to the sleeping baby. "You're a natural," she said.

"Cuddling is easy."

"What's hard?"

He hesitated, then settled on the truth. "Remembering."

She made a sound of sympathy but didn't make eye contact, for which he was grateful.

"Mary Ann took care of Kyle," he said into the silence. "I thought the most important thing in my life should be providing for my family, so I gave more time to my work than my family. I wasn't part of Kyle's everyday life, especially as a baby. It'll be different this time."

"Good. Although apparently you're a very busy man, much in demand. From what I saw on the Internet, you're at the top of your field."

"Not the top, but I do okay. It's amazing how an oddball thing like being a recluse can have such impact. People are curious, which gets my foot in the door, so to speak. Then they like my designs."

"How do you meet with clients?"

"They come here. I think they're disappointed because I don't have a wild, overgrown beard and a crazy gleam in my eyes. My partner handles the engineering aspect—someone has to be on-site during construction. And a business manager handles the staff. I design."

Daniel wriggled. Almost instantly he started to cry—loudly. Demandingly.

"I'll fix a bottle," Heath said, starting to pass the baby to Cassie.

"Or I could fix a bottle and you could change his diaper," she said, challenge in her eyes.

"Simple engineering."

"Go for it. I'll warm the formula." She pressed a kiss to the baby's head. "Daddy needs to learn sometime, doesn't he, Danny Boy?"

Danny Boy. At the endearment Heath almost pressed a kiss to *her* head. He didn't know what fates were at work when he called her boss and got her instead, but he was grateful.

Somehow he didn't think Quinn Gerard would've said yes to being a temporary nanny.

Six

"**I** think you should put the baby monitor in my room," Cassie argued at eleven o'clock that night. They'd just settled Danny into his bassinet for what they hoped would be a couple hours of uninterrupted sleep.

"I'm his father."

"I'm the help."

"Reluctant help," he said placidly.

She tapped her toe. It would drive her crazy staying in bed knowing Heath was up taking care of the baby. Call it maternal instinct, call it selfishness, call it a little crazy—she wanted to get up with Danny during the night. Frankly she wanted the bassinet put in her room.

On the other hand, she would need her light on, which might shorten his sleep cycle, or at least not allow him to get used to sleeping when it was dark. He needed to learn to take his bottle then go back to sleep at night, not have playtime.

"We can take turns," Heath said.

"How?"

"I'll put the monitor near my bedroom door. We can both keep our doors open. I'll get up with him the first time. You can take the second."

If she left her door open he would know what a coward she could be, but since it was probably as much of a concession as he was going to make, she agreed to it. "We'll give it a shot."

"Magnanimous of you."

She laughed. He hadn't laughed yet, had barely smiled, yet he'd warmed up considerably with her. Maybe she didn't have to worry about there not being enough joy in Danny's life, after all. She only needed to make sure he would get out into the world—with his father, not a nanny.

"Well, good night, then," she said.

"Good night."

She closed her door. By the time she'd gotten ready for bed and opened her door again, he was already in bed. His door was partly open, his room dark. She hadn't noticed the silence of the house all day, even when Danny was quiet and she and Heath weren't talking. Now it seemed silent again.

Which was reasonable, of course, but it was a strange silence, not a comfortable nighttime silence. Just the different environment, she decided. And the doors were open, which seemed too intimate for two almost strangers. He could walk across the hall and into her room while she slept and she wouldn't know.

Cassie climbed into bed, the bathroom light spilling into her room. She closed her eyes, willing herself to relax.

She could walk across the hall while *he* slept, too, and he wouldn't know, either.

The idea intrigued her. What was it about him that appealed to her? His looks, of course. His intelligence. Success—that counted a lot with her. It wouldn't matter what job he had, just that he was successful in it and content with the job he did.

He'd been understating his reputation earlier. She'd learned he was one of the premier designers of skyscrapers in the country, maybe the world. He was sought after. People waited a long time for him to even consult with them on an initial design.

How was he going to incorporate a baby into that life? Especially without a wife. A nanny would be a big help, but it wasn't the same thing.

Maybe once he started getting out of the house he would open up emotionally again, meet a woman, date. Get married. Have more children.

She looked around the guest room. She didn't know much about furniture, but everything looked expensive. Rich woods polished to a gleam. A handmade quilt on the bed in a pattern she didn't know the name of but was probably something he picked up on a trip somewhere. The art on the walls wasn't bought at a garage sale, like hers.

Still, like the rest of the house, the room needed fresh flowers and that certain touch that comes from having someone around who cared about such things. She bought herself fresh flowers every Friday for her studio apartment, and considered them a necessity not a luxury.

Cassie smoothed the quilt, tracing the pattern with her fingertips. If she'd been at home on a normal Saturday night, she would've either been working—surveillance, probably—or going to dinner then maybe out to a club with friends. The sameness of it all was getting to her. She was twenty-nine years old, and restless. However, her job required more than a sixty-hour work week most of the time, and she didn't know if any man would accept the amount of time she put in. She'd lost a few potential boyfriends because of it. She hadn't cared. Until recently.

A light tapping on her door startled her.

"Can't sleep?" he asked, not entering her room, not even looking in.

He wouldn't know that she'd been trying to sleep. She sat up and grabbed her notebook from the nightstand, making it seem as if she'd been writing in it.

"Come in," she said.

He wore a T-shirt and pajama bottoms, as covered up as she was in her pajamas, yet it seemed too familiar.

"You can't sleep, either?" she asked.

He shook his head. He didn't come into the room but stayed at the doorway, leaning a shoulder against it. "What you said earlier about being in foster homes—how old were you?"

She pulled up her knees and rested her back against the headboard. "Nine."

"What happened to put you there?"

"My mother OD'd when I was five. My dad wasn't in the picture. My grandfather took me in, but he died when I was nine." She saw sympathy in his eyes and didn't want it. "It's in the past, Heath. Over and done."

"How many homes?"

She answered but had no plans to elaborate. "Seven."

"Were you a problem child?"

"You could say that. I've changed."

"I'm not sure." He smiled so she knew he was joking. "Depends on the circumstances. You jerked my chain, Mr. Raven, friend of Senator Sterling."

"I'm not sorry."

Over the monitor they could hear Danny fuss. She threw back her blankets.

"My turn," he reminded her.

"But I'm awake, too. He shouldn't need to eat yet, so maybe just a little rocking back to sleep. I'm better at that than you are."

"Bragger."

"It's true."

They faced off. She finally smiled. "How about if we go together?"

"What a novel idea."

She laughed quietly, then hesitated a moment. Even though her pajamas weren't see-through, it would be apparent she was not wearing a bra. The only other option was to get dressed, which seemed silly and obvious and immature, even. For all intents and purposes they were doing a job together, and that was all.

"He's sounding very unhappy," Heath said, his brows raised.

She stopped debating with herself. Her priority was Danny, after all. "Well, let's go cheer him up."

Heath knew Cassie hated not being the one to hold Danny, but he wasn't about to let her take charge. This was his son, and she wouldn't be there forever. He needed to learn how to care for Danny on his own, especially if he decided he only wanted day help.

Danny's crying was winding down. Heath paced the living room, bouncing him lightly, making soothing sounds. Maybe it had taken him longer than it would have taken Cassie, but Danny had finally settled down. Every once in a while he hiccuped but he was almost dead weight. Heath decided if he talked and Danny didn't wake up, he would be asleep enough to put back to bed.

He wanted to know more about her childhood. His own parents may have been a little on the flaky side, but at least he'd had a steady, loving upbringing. "Why wasn't your father in the picture?"

"I have no idea who he was. He was not named on the birth certificate, nor was I ever told a name."

Heath sat across from her on the sofa. "How was it living with your grandfather?"

She smiled, reminiscence in her eyes. "He was old and sweet. He'd lost touch with my mom years earlier, and didn't even know that I existed, so he was a bit bewildered when the Florida child welfare people tracked him down here in San Francisco. I know I was a huge responsibility for him at a time in his life he didn't need any. Look, there was good and bad in my upbringing, as there is in everyone's."

He heard the dismissal in her voice. A touchy subject for her. What happened? he wondered. If it had been a good experience, she would've said so. "Did you go to college?"

"Yes. I liked school."

She was stingy with her answers. It made him want to know more. "You were a good student."

"I decided I could be just as successful as anyone else. Maybe my hurdles were bigger than some, but they were also smaller than others. I didn't want to become a stereotype."

"A stereotype? You mean as a product of the system?"

"Yes. I fought to stay at the same high school for all four years. Can we change the subject?"

"I'm interested because we lived such different lives. Why are you so defensive?"

"Because I don't look back."

The way she plucked at her pajama bottoms led him to believe there was a lot more to say. How much more could he push her tonight? "What was your major in college?"

"Criminal justice."

"Why?"

"I wanted to be a lawyer."

"Why didn't you?"

"I ran out of money for law school, so I took the job as an investigator for Oberman, Steele and Jenkins. I ended up enjoying it. Didn't have to stay cooped up in an office or a courtroom all day."

He wondered about that. He would bet she still had dreams of becoming a lawyer, probably defending children's rights. "How did you support yourself through college?"

"Jobs. Lots of jobs."

He thought about his own college life. He'd gotten a full scholarship, only having to work for spending money.

She said nothing for a few seconds then angled toward him. "Danny's sound asleep. I think we should get some sleep ourselves while we can. You never know how long the quiet will last."

He didn't feel tired at all. He wanted to hear about her life, and how she'd carved out her own future. His path had been so much easier, with hardly a bump in any road. Except for Kyle—

"You're right." He stood. "Let's hope he lasts longer than a half hour this time."

He felt Cassie walking behind him to the nursery. He put Danny carefully into the bassinet, which was in the crib. Danny barely moved.

"Next time you can hold him. Even if I'm up," Heath said.

"You figure we're going to come to fists over him?" she whispered, a smile in her voice, as they both leaned over the crib.

Heath turned his head toward her. She was barely a foot away. A sliver of light from the hall illuminated her face enough that she was all intriguing shadows. She went as still as a statue. He inched closer. Her gaze dropped to his mouth and lingered. She smelled of soap and toothpaste. He wanted to put his palms along her face, bring her close, touch his lips to hers. Slip his hands under her pajama top, feel her skin—

She straightened abruptly. "I don't— I mean…"

He pulled back. "Right. Yes. Of course." What the hell was he doing? Wasn't that how he got into this predicament in the first place? Well, not exactly, but giving his long-starved libido free rein had something to do with it. He couldn't kiss her, couldn't make that mistake.

"I'll see you later," she said then hurried off ahead of him.

He waited a minute, following more slowly, letting her go ahead without the potentially awkward moment of them standing outside their rooms.

An hour later Danny woke up. Heath let Cassie take over. The next time, two hours later, she slept—or pretended to sleep—while he fed and changed Danny.

As he walked Danny to sleep he glanced toward the stairs, wondering if she was awake and thinking about the kiss that had almost happened, that would have happened had she not stepped back, showing much more self-control than he had.

He really needed to get out of the house, he decided with a laugh at himself.

When he went to bed a few minutes later, he noticed her bedroom light was still on. He stood outside his bedroom for a few seconds, in case she called out to him.

She didn't, and he went into his increasingly lonely bedroom, wondering at all the changes in his life and what would come next. He was ready for the adventure.

Seven

Cassie didn't usually have leisurely Sundays, so the idea of having nothing to do but cook, eat and play with Danny seemed like a vacation. She hadn't taken one of those in a long time, either, although Quinn informed her she would be required to take three weeks a year, no argument, no postponing.

She hummed to herself as she flipped pancakes on the griddle to add to those already staying warm in the oven. She'd heard the shower running upstairs, so she figured Heath would make his way downstairs soon.

She needed to calm herself down before he got there. She'd almost kissed him last night. Almost shouldn't count, maybe normally it didn't. But last night it counted. She had a job to do. He was the client.

And yet earlier she had seen his gaze drift down her

a few times, not blatantly, but enough to feel his interest and to figure he knew she wasn't wearing a bra under her pajamas. Of course, she'd checked him out, too, and looked him over pretty thoroughly.

So she was nervous this morning. So what?

She drew a settling breath. Just slightly panicked, she looked around the room. Was she pushing too much by opening every drape and blind? If he didn't like it, she'd already figured out a way to get him to leave the blinds open. She'd also set the back porch table for breakfast. Too pushy, again? Probably. She didn't care. Whatever it took to help him get back to living. Danny needed that from him. What was he going to do—fire her? At least it would be a distraction from the almost-kiss.

It was almost eleven o'clock. Danny hadn't slept much during the night but had been asleep now for over two hours. Every fifteen minutes or so she would tiptoe in and check on him. He must've worn himself out finally.

She heard Heath coming down the staircase, his footfalls slow and steady. Her heart rate picked up. She wanted to see his face when he saw the outside light pouring in, to gauge for herself his reaction.

He came into the kitchen, his eyes riveted on the view.

She pulled the warm platter filled with pancakes and bacon from the oven to add the final pancakes. "Breakfast is ready," she said, her pulse tripping, when he remained silent for too long. "I thought we could eat on the back porch."

He met her gaze then didn't break the connection for several long seconds. "You've really moved in."

She didn't miss all the implications of his words. "That's what you hired me to do."

"It's my house, Cassie. My choices."

She went to the refrigerator and took out the fruit plate she'd put together. "Well, I don't want to alarm you, but Danny looks a little jaundiced to me. He needs sunlight." Although not much could break through his forest, anyway.

He gave her a look of disbelief, but would he call her on it?

"Do you drink coffee?" she asked quickly, not letting him take the conversation further.

"Yes."

Tension continued to build, evident in the way his back went straighter and he crossed his arms. His jaw twitched.

"Let's fill our plates here then take them outside," she said, undaunted. "Everything will get too cold otherwise."

She grabbed the carafe of coffee she'd already brewed, and added cream and sugar and maple syrup, placing everything on a tray. "Butter for your pancakes?" she asked lightly, as if not noticing how distant he looked.

"No. Thanks."

"Would you mind carrying the tray out? I'll fix our plates."

She nudged the edge of the tray against his midsection. He grasped the handles. "I know what you're doing," he said, his eyes almost a forest-green they'd darkened so much.

Well, she never thought he was stupid. "Is it all right?"

He made her wait an interminable amount of time. "I'm not sure yet."

She rubbed his arm. His warmth penetrated his sleeve to heat her palm. Her heart raced.

"This is a bad idea," he said quietly.

She pulled her hand back, disappointed but also surprised. She thought she'd begun to understand him.

"I don't mean your touching me," he said. "Although that's part of it...." He let the sentence fade away. "I need you here. I don't want to do anything that would make you feel like you had to leave before everything is settled. I know you're here because of Danny."

"Partly," she said honestly. "I'm always a champion for kids. But...."

"But?"

"There's you, too." She couldn't say more than that, because she didn't know what more to say. The jury was out on him. She only knew that she was drawn to him for a lot of complicated reasons and a few simple ones.

"I'm not attracted to you because I've been without a woman for so long," he said. "You need to know that. Women come and go in my life, business contacts, like you. I've never felt this—this need, especially this fast."

"So, we need to be careful."

"Yes," he said quietly.

"So, no touching."

He hesitated. "I don't want to make rules. Do you?"

No. She didn't need the guilt that would come if they *broke* any rules. She shook her head.

He seemed to relax all at once. "Okay. We'll take it slow and easy. Deal with the issues at hand first."

"Then when life settles down, we'll see where it goes from there," she said. Although he was wrong, she thought. "Slow and easy" wasn't going to work for them. The tension between them ratcheted up another notch hourly, it seemed. "Breakfast is getting cold."

Awkwardness accompanied the meal, not only because of their discussion but because he was sitting outdoors. As they finished their second cups of coffee she closed her eyes, wishing the sun could find its way through the gloom surrounding his house.

"What would you be doing today if you weren't here?" he asked.

"If I'm not working, I spend Sundays volunteering at the O'Connor Children's Home."

"What do you do?"

"I counsel mostly. Been-there, done-that kind of thing."

"They'll be missing you today. Maybe you should—"

"No. I called in already. They know they can't count on me every week. My job takes me out of town quite a bit, but it's also just a matter of working very long hours."

"You enjoy it, though."

"No question. ARC takes on such a variety of cases. Well, maybe that's not exactly it. It's the clients that make it so fascinating. Celebrities, executives, politicians— they have a high-powered list, and the work is rarely routine." She looked at him over the rim of her mug. "I heard you'd actually wanted my boss for your case."

"I generally get the person at the top."

"But you got me instead."

He toasted her. "Even better."

"Thanks."

"I don't think your boss would've moved in and helped out with the baby."

She thought he smiled. His eyes seemed to twinkle. "You wouldn't have asked him," she countered.

"True." He set his mug on the table and leaned back. "This has been nice."

"I'm glad."

"Were you worried?"

"Nah. I'm a pretty good cook when I set my mind to it." She smiled. She knew what he meant, but chose not to respond to it. Of course she'd been worried that he would balk at sitting outdoors, but worry never stopped her from doing what was necessary.

Through the portable baby monitor they heard Daniel fuss.

"I'll clean up the kitchen," Heath said. "You can get the baby."

She pushed back her chair. "You just don't want diaper duty."

He grinned.

Silence swooped in like a huge, noiseless, hovering bird. Her heart stopped. Triumph grabbed hold of her. She'd done that. She'd made him smile like that.

Now she needed to figure out how to do it again, and again, and again.

A couple hours later Heath wandered over to a window in his office and lifted a slat. He couldn't see Cassie and Danny, who were out enjoying a walk. Cassie had invited Heath along, but he wanted to use the time to get some work done. Or so he told her.

It was mostly true. He had plenty of work to do, although not much interest. That was a first.

He walked to the other end of the office and lifted a

blind there then spotted her. She was standing still, although swinging side to side. Heath wondered if Danny was awake.

He dropped the slat and stepped away, tunneling his fingers through his hair. His jaw hurt. Everything hurt. Stress was his constant companion, although not for a few minutes now and then today.

Cassie relaxed him just by being there. Except when she aroused him just by being there.

If he joined her and Danny outside he might be able to touch her, to put a hand under her arm when she came up the stairs. She wouldn't pull away over a simple touch like that, would she?

He liked how she stood up to him, liked the fire in her eyes when she did—and the way her posture changed. She stood a little taller, put her shoulders back and her chin up. A sexy stance, emphasizing her breasts. Yeah, he definitely wanted to join them in their walk.

He made the decision too late. The front door opened and closed.

He went down the stairs anyway to greet them. Danny's eyes were open. She plopped him in Heath's arms, said, "I'll be right back," then headed toward the downstairs powder room.

He watched her until she disappeared, his gaze on her very sexy rear. He imagined his hands there, lifting her higher against him as they kissed—

He stopped the thought cold. Ideas like that could only lead to complications.

"Did you enjoy your walk?" he asked his tiny son, turning toward the living room, his attention solely on Danny. He didn't see any yellow tinge to Danny's complexion. The open drapes made it seem almost as if they were outdoors, which had been his original goal when he designed the house for the property, and why he'd named it *Raven's View*. He didn't focus on the surroundings, however, but on Danny. "She's something, isn't she?" he whispered to the boy. "A natural-born mom. And one beautiful woman."

Danny arched his back. His tiny hands came out from under the blanket. He tucked them under his chin. Heath bent down and kissed the little fingers curled into fists, then his forehead, then each cheek, as his baby scent imprinted on Heath's brain. An image of Kyle flashed in his mind. His eyes burned. His throat ached. He barely remembered him as an infant, an unbearably sad realization. As a little boy he'd had hair as blond as Mary Ann's, but Heath's nose and mouth and green eyes.

Heath would've liked to compare the brothers, but he couldn't because Mary Ann had taken all the photo albums, leaving him nothing. Nothing except memories, and those were tainted by the final one. *Dad-dy!* Kyle's voice haunted him. Would always haunt him.

"Did you get some work done?"

Cassie had come up beside him.

He didn't want her to see him like this, but he couldn't escape, either. He lifted his gaze to her.

"Oh. Oh, Heath."

The sympathy in her eyes was like a gut punch. She lifted a hand. He pulled back. Pushy as always she didn't back away. After a second she stroked his hair, her touch soothing. Too soothing. He didn't want to break down with her. He hadn't broken down. It was going to be ugly when—if—he did.

"Don't," he said quietly.

As usual she didn't listen to him. She went up on tip-toe and pressed her lips to his, lightly, just a brush, re-ally. He cupped the back of her head as she would have pulled away and drew out the kiss a little bit longer, then he wrapped an arm around her and pulled her against him, so that her head rested against his shoulder. Ah, the simple pleasure of human touch, of human warmth. It had been so long. So very long.

"Thank you for being here," he said. "I'm not sure how well I would've done on my own."

"You would be fine. You're quite relaxed with him."

Because you're here, he thought, knowing it was the truth. How did single parents do it? Well, he was about to find out, and he probably had more financial resour-ces than most single parents. But paying for help didn't relieve the anxiety of raising a child alone.

He let go of Cassie. "Do you have work you should be doing?" he asked.

"A little. Most has to wait until businesses are open tomorrow. I'll work the next time Danny naps, which should be soon."

"You should nap. We both should."

"You're probably right. Are you ready for some lunch first?"

"You don't have to wait on me."

"I know." She smiled. "We'll barbecue tonight. Let man build fire." She grunted.

He smiled back as she walked away, her braid swing-ing back and forth, brushing the small of her back. He wanted to rest his hand there, in that gently curved hollow.

Too much fantasizing, he thought, not following her.

Time for a cold shower of sorts. He and Danny would watch the Forty-niners play on television. It was never too soon for a boy's first football game.

Eight

After a short nap Cassie walked down the hallway and stood in the doorway of Heath's office. His back was to her, his attention focused on his computer monitor. The blinds were still shut. What will it take? she wondered. Why won't he open them? This was the one room she wouldn't push him about. Plus he probably wouldn't let her, anyway.

She didn't expect him to take leaps and bounds out of the emotional trench he'd been stuck in for years, but opening blinds seemed like a baby step.

She wondered whether she should say hello or go off and do some work herself. What she really wanted was to bring her computer into his office and work where she could see him, talk to him. Touch him. Especially that. It was getting harder and harder not to.

"You can come in," he said, turning around, surprising her. "Did you sleep?"

"I did. How about you?" She hoped her need didn't show in her eyes as she took a seat at his worktable.

"I got enough to keep going." He typed a few keystrokes, then gave her his full attention. "What's next, Cassie?"

"Um, pork tenderloin. Fresh asparagus that we can grill, too. Red potatoes, which I'll oven roast with some rosemary and olive oil."

"I meant with Danny, but that sounds good."

She smiled. "Sorry. I'm hungry." She grabbed a pen from the tabletop and tapped it against her palm. "I've got the name of a reputable agency about getting a nanny. I'll contact them tomorrow. You need an attorney to spell out the legal details, but I'm sure you'll need DNA testing to prove paternity. There are some firms where you can mail samples in and get results in a week, but you'll want the chain of custody of the samples for your proof. It takes a little longer. Do you have a family attorney?"

"Yes. How do I get a copy of the birth certificate?"

"It'll be sent to the Office of Vital Records from wherever it was Eva gave birth."

"Will I be able to access it?"

"She can't have put you down as the father, but don't worry about it. I've got a great relationship with that office. I'll work it out."

Heath frowned. "Why couldn't she put me down as the father?"

"State law says the father's name can be reported on the birth certificate only if the parents are legally married or if the father agrees to give up his right to challenge paternity."

"But I'm not challenging that right."

"Did you sign a Declaration of Paternity form?"

"I didn't know such a thing existed."

Eva should have known, though, Cassie thought. "As I said, we'll get it worked out. It would be helpful to at least talk with Eva."

She decided to start dinner, because what she really wanted was to bombard him with questions. To understand him. To get a sense that he would return to the land of the living. She tossed the pen on the table as she stood. "You'll call the lawyer in the morning? Unless he's also such a good friend he would come here on a Sunday."

He smiled. "He is, but I'll call him tomorrow morning instead. You seem to resent my contacts, Cassie."

"I envy them. Anyway, he'll probably draw up a new document for Eva to sign, if you hear from her again." She walked away.

"I expect I'll hear from her."

At the doorway Cassie faced him. He sounded so sure. "Why?"

"Just a gut instinct. Maybe the way she looked at Danny before she ran off."

"How was that?"

"Torn. Sad."

Cassie's suspicions sprang up again. She doubted things were going to work out the way Heath wanted. Either the baby wasn't his, after all, or Eva would take him back. Cassie needed to decide how to lay the groundwork for those possibilities with Heath.

She leaned against the jamb. "What was she like during the pregnancy?"

"How do you mean?"

"Was she content? Excited? Afraid? Had she wanted to end the pregnancy? Did she seem to be looking forward to being a mother?"

"The pregnancy wasn't planned and we weren't married. It didn't exactly make for an ideal situation."

"I understand that."

He stood, too, and came close to Cassie. "She didn't tell me she was pregnant until after she could have terminated it, and we didn't talk about if she'd even considered it. If she had asked for my input I would've asked her to keep the baby and give him to me."

"And her attitude?"

"I would say she wasn't excited but not afraid, either. I don't know how to describe it. She was different after she was pregnant, but I expected her to be different. The way she took off at the end stunned me. It was way out of character."

"She seemed to want so little of you, other than money."

He stood a little straighter. His expression hardened. "That's not entirely true. She wanted to share the pregnancy with me."

"Maybe because you needed to share it, and she was reacting to your need."

"Maybe."

"Then she disappeared."

"Yeah. And now there's pushy Cassie Miranda."

"I'm looking out for Danny."

"I figured that out for myself. You don't have the world's best poker face when it comes to my son."

But was Danny his son? Cassie wondered. "Kids deserve—"

He put a finger to her lips for a moment. "Yes, they do. I'm trying, Cassie. I know you haven't told me…half? A tenth? Of what you went through in foster care, but I know a lot of it wasn't good. I hope you'll share it with me sometime."

She'd blocked much of it and never wanted to relive it. But plenty of kids had been in worse situations than she. "I wasn't sexually abused," she said, giving him that much. But trust? That was a different issue. As hard as she tried, putting her faith in anyone other than herself was next to impossible, at least *complete* faith.

"I'm glad to hear that."

"I—" she jerked a thumb over her shoulder "—need to start dinner."

Still she didn't move. Neither did he. They looked into each other's eyes, searching for…what?

"What happened to you in those homes?" Heath asked, his hand brushing hers.

"Give me a half hour to get things going, then you can start the grill," she said. She spun away from him.

"We're quite a pair, aren't we, Cassie?"

"Yeah." She got the word out but that was all. She hurried down the stairs, her boot heels pounding. Danny let out a wail. She detoured into his room, swept him into her arms and held him close, resting her cheek against his head.

She was already in too deep with this child—and this man. She shouldn't stay.

But she couldn't go.

Would she ever be able to?

"You're right. This document would never hold up in court," Heath's lawyer said the next afternoon before taking a bite of pasta salad. Kerwin Rudyard had given up his lunch hour to drive to Heath's house. Cassie had gone into the city to work but hadn't gotten back in time to meet Kerwin.

"Then I need you to draw up a document that will," Heath said.

"I can draw it up, but you need to know this will be an uphill battle. She's going to have rights, if she changes her mind."

"I assumed as much. I want to protect Danny as much as I can. Could she take him away entirely?"

"Let's not concern ourselves with that just yet, Heath. One step at a time. First step, a lab technician will come take samples for DNA testing. We want to be sure of the chain of custody, so you don't have to repeat any steps in future and slow down the process."

"Yes, Cassie told me that."

"Cassie?"

"Cassie Miranda, a P.I. with ARC Security and Investigations."

"I'm familiar with the agency. You're paying top dollar but you're getting top performance."

"I can tell."

"I've known Quinn Oliver for years, before we knew his name was Quinn." He chuckled. "One of the best undercovers— Well, anyway, you're in good hands."

"I'm sure of it. What's the second step?"

"You need to find Eva."

"Cassie's working on it. Can you get the birth certificate?"

"If you won't go in person to the Office of Vital Records, I'll need a sworn statement from you, notarized, but not until the DNA testing proves you're the father. The birth certificate probably can't have reached their office yet, so we'll deal with that later. A lot can happen between now and then." Kerwin folded up his napkin and laid it beside his empty plate. "Thanks for lunch."

"Thanks for coming. It was great seeing you, although we could've handled this over the phone." He followed the silver-haired man to the door. They'd known each other for fifteen years. Heath had forgotten how much he enjoyed Kerwin's company.

"We could've, but I wanted to see for myself how you were doing." He cocked his head. "You're better."

"Getting there. As much as I ever will, anyway."

"Have you forgiven yourself?"

Heath shook his head. There was nothing to say.

Kerwin started to walk away, then turned back. "Did you hear that Mary Ann is getting married?"

The news barely registered on his emotional Richter scale. "We don't stay in touch."

"No, I guess you wouldn't. Oh, something else—who becomes Danny's guardian if something happens to you?"

Heath's mind went blank.

"Think about it," Kerwin said into the silence.

Heath moved into the yard when his friend drove off, seeking a small pool of sunshine. He closed his eyes and lifted his face. Pleasure assaulted him—a healing warmth, the tempting lure of one of the most basic needs in life, to feel the sun on your face. Peace seeped into him, even with all the unknowns ahead.

He heard a car approach, saw Cassie coming up the driveway. He needed to do something about the over-growth. It had gotten thick enough to scratch car paint. Why hadn't anyone said anything?

Which was a rhetorical question. No one criticized him. Only Cassie had come close, by opening blinds without asking him first, her criticism silent but obvious.

He watched her get out of her car and come toward him. Damn but he loved to watch her walk. A slow pace might be considered sexy by some people, but her long strides and quick pace turned him on. A lot.

"Did you get everything taken care of at the office?" he asked.

"I got footwork done. I'll make some phone calls from here. I want to touch base with Eva's roommate, Darcy, again. She's our best hope. If Eva gets in touch with anyone, I think it'll be Darcy." She set down her briefcase and took off her jacket. "How's Danny?"

"He was cranky for a while when Kerwin first got here. He took a bottle and went back to sleep. Been down for half an hour."

"What did your lawyer have to say?"

"Pretty much repeated everything you said." *Except he wants to know who would be Danny's guardian.* "And he's heard of you."

"Is that a good thing?"

"He said your firm has one of the worst reputations in the city, and what the hell was I doing hiring incompetents?"

She looked surprised, then she laughed. "You made a joke!"

"I've been known to, on occasion."

"Keep it up." She lifted her face to the meager ray of sunshine. "There's nothing like September in San Francisco."

Bathed in sunlight she seemed to have an angelic aura, yet he knew she was tough. Maybe *strong* was a better word. Maybe both. Except for her devotion to Danny, she didn't let much emotion show. Because she was being professional or because her past had blighted her emotionally?

"I contacted the agency about hiring a nanny," she said casually but her gaze was direct. "I made an appointment for you tomorrow with the director. She'll be here around ten o'clock so you can interview each other."

His gut clenched. He wasn't ready for that. He didn't want to share his home with anyone—except Cassie. "Great," he said, turning toward the house. "Thanks."

"We'll find someone you're comfortable with," she said behind him.

He nodded, and kept walking.

Danny wouldn't stop crying. They walked and walked, talked and talked. Cassie even sneaked him into another room and sang to him. Nothing helped. Finally she said to Heath, "I'm taking him for a drive."

"No."

"It should calm him down. Most babies respond to it." She knew he didn't want Danny out of his sight— she was also counting on it. He would come along. Take a drive with them. Open up his world a little.

"I'm a good driver," she said, pretending to let him think that's what he was worried about.

Danny let out a wail. "All right, already," Heath said. "A ride. But I'm going, too. And don't for one minute think I don't know what you're doing."

She liked him more every hour. His confinement would've broken a lesser man, but he'd dealt with his grief in his own way. She respected that, even as she respected the take-charge man who refused to let her be boss.

They had put the base of his car seat in her car the day before, in case they needed to go somewhere in a hurry, so all they had to do was lock his carrier into the base and they were ready to go.

Heath climbed into the passenger seat.

Cassie tried not to look at him, except she could see his fingers pressing into his thighs as she started the engine and pulled out. She wouldn't ask if he was okay. If he wasn't, she expected him to tell her, but she wouldn't give him an easy out.

It wasn't quite seven o'clock. There was daylight left. She wanted him to see what he'd been missing.

Danny quieted down fast, so fast that she was afraid Heath would want to go back home, but he didn't say so. Except for giving her directions, he remained silent.

"I'd forgotten how beautiful it is," he said finally, his voice hushed as they came to a spot that revealed a spectacular view of the city and bay.

She decided not to trespass on his reawakening by responding. They dropped down into the shopping district.

"How about an ice-cream sundae?" she asked.

He hesitated. "Okay."

She didn't see a parking place close to the ice-cream

parlor, so she entered a public lot. Heath lifted the baby carrier out.

"Let's go watch the ferry come in," he said, pointing toward the bay.

They leaned against a railing to await the boat as drifts of diesel fuel merged with the distinctive salty scent of the bay. After a few minutes commuters began to exit the ferry.

Cassie hadn't spent a lot of time in Sausalito. Even though she made a very good income, the properties were too expensive for her—or more than she was willing to pay. She knew the value of living off half her income and saving the rest, just in case. But she enjoyed the community, well-known for its art festival every Labor Day, even though she hadn't ever attended. Big crowds made her edgy.

"You're not very talkative," Heath said into her musings.

"Just enjoying the evening."

"You haven't even asked how I'm doing."

She rested an elbow against the railing, eyeing him. "You're not exhibiting signs of imminent panic."

"You'd be surprised. But three days ago I couldn't have done this much."

"Don't give me any credit. This is all your own doing. And maybe Danny's." She tucked Danny's blanket more closely around him as the breeze picked up. "Does it feel real yet?"

"Danny, you mean?"

She nodded.

"I'm afraid to let it feel real. What if Eva wants him back?"

Good. He *had* been thinking about it. "You can't hold back just because the situation may change." She was as guilty of that as anyone. She'd learned to hold back every time she was placed with a new foster parent. She knew she wouldn't be there long. Why get attached? And it was easier for her foster parent to let go if Cassie didn't seem to care, either.

"Danny's mine," Heath said, breaking into her thoughts. "But I know I might be facing a battle."

Maybe he's yours. Should she say that? Not now, she decided. Not at this critical moment. "Don't give up."

He laid a hand against her shoulder, then lifted it to her cheek. "I won't."

She stopped herself just before she leaned into him, wanting more, needing more. She turned toward the shops, breaking the physical contact with him. "I hear some hot fudge sauce calling my name."

They kept their conversation light after that. No revelations. No dark questions. No reliving the past. Just a man, a woman and a baby, brought together under unusual circumstances but finding things in common.

"Do you want to drive back?" she asked when they reached her car after sunset.

"No. Thanks."

Danny continued to sleep, Heath said nothing. The quiet soothed Cassie, and she ignored the feeling that it was just the calm before the storm.

Nine

Heath jerked awake. He lay in his bed listening, but didn't hear anything. He glanced at the clock, noted it was almost midnight. Danny should be awake soon, wanting to eat. That must've been what woke Heath up.

He closed his eyes but couldn't get back to sleep, was surprised that he'd fallen asleep that early to begin with. His lack of sleep was catching up, he supposed.

He got out of bed and wandered to his window. A car was parked at the top of his driveway. A car that looked like—

He ran from the room and into Cassie's, noting her light was on, but she was sound asleep. "Cassie." He didn't touch her, only said her name in a hurry, wanting to get back to his window.

"What?" She seemed instantly awake.

"There's a car in my driveway. It looks like Eva's."

She tossed the blankets aside and jumped out of bed.

"You can see from my bedroom."

"Why would I do that?" She grabbed her briefcase then jogged down the staircase ahead of him. "Did you see someone get out of the car?"

"No, but they had time to get out before I even saw the car."

"I don't like that no one has rung the bell." She peeked out the tall glass window next to the front door. "I don't see anyone. No, wait. Someone is in the car. Two people. I can see their silhouettes. Can't tell what gender they are."

Heath looked over her shoulder. Cassie set her briefcase on the floor, opened it and pulled out her gun.

"What are you doing?"

"Being prepared."

"What if it's teenagers making out?"

"Then I won't shoot." She turned and grinned at him. "I know what I'm doing."

They watched for a while longer. Sure enough, the pair inside the car kissed. Then the car doors opened.

"Oh, no," Heath said.

"What? Do you know them?"

"Yeah." He sighed and opened the front door, flipped on the porch light.

"Earthie!"

He closed his eyes at the sound of his mother's voice. She came flying across the yard and straight into his arms. She wore— He didn't know what the hell she was wearing. One of her usual hippie, throwback, long dresses and sandals, her long gray hair loose and frizzy.

His father loped along behind her, his smile broad, his own gray hair pulled into a ponytail.

Heath patted his mother's back, then released her to hug his father.

"Where's my grandson?"

"Asleep, Mom." Danny started to cry. "Well, he was. It's feeding time. Why didn't you call?"

"We wanted to surprise you. My goodness, he's got a healthy set of lungs."

"He lets us know when he's hungry," Heath said. "This is Cassie Miranda. She's a friend of mine. Cassie, these are my parents, Crystal and Journey Raven."

He was glad he'd told her their names already. She didn't cringe at all. Or laugh.

"It's very nice to meet you," Cassie said.

Cassie dwarfed his mother, who was just shy of five feet tall, his father a foot taller.

"You can go get him, if you want, Mom," Heath said, ending the polite chitchat that usually accompanied introductions.

His mother followed the sound, staking her claim to the baby. His father had a hand on her shoulder, touching, as always. Heath had never seen a couple touch each other as much as his parents did.

Cassie mouthed, "Earthie?" to him as they fell in step behind his parents.

He shrugged. She elbowed him in the ribs, making him smile.

"There's a story there," she said.

"Not a big one. Earth Heathcliff Raven. That's my full name."

"Say that ten times fast." Her eyes sparkled.

"You're biting your lip."

"Am not. Can't talk and bite my lip at the same time."

They entered the nursery side by side. He realized suddenly that he was relaxed, a rarity when his parents were around. His mother, at least. He loved her but she got on his nerves faster than—

"He's using disposable diapers!" Heath heard her declare, which she'd unerringly found.

"And so it begins," he muttered to Cassie, who grinned.

"I'll warm a bottle," he called out to his mother, heading toward the kitchen, taking Cassie by the hand.

Cassie took a seat at the counter as he ran hot water into a bowl. Her eyes no longer smiled.

"What?" he asked.

"You don't need me here anymore."

Her words slammed into him. "We still need to find Eva. Track down the birth certificate."

"That's the job you hired me to do. I don't have to live here to do my job. You needed help with Danny. You will have help from your parents."

He didn't have an argument for that—not one he could say out loud, anyway, without scaring her off. He met her serious gaze for several long seconds. "Stay," he said finally. "Please."

"You only have one guest room set up."

"They can have my room. I'll sleep on the couch in my office."

"Why would you do that?"

Because life is better when you're around. "Because my mother will take over, otherwise."

"You mean, she won't if I'm here because she might think she's invading my turf?"

"Exactly."

"But I'm not. She can see I'm not. We don't sleep together."

"She wouldn't know that. She would think we're being considerate."

He heard his parents approaching. Danny was fussing but not crying. His mother always had a magic touch with babies.

"Bottle, please." Crystal held out her hand.

"I have a feeling I'm never going to hold my son again," Heath said as he passed her the bottle.

"Of course you will. When I'm gone." She smiled sweetly.

Cassie lifted her brows as if to say, "See? You don't need me."

"You must be exhausted," Cassie said to his parents. "I'll get my stuff and take off."

"Oh, no. We wouldn't hear of it," his father said.

"It's fine, really. Heath, would you join me upstairs for a minute, please?"

He went with her to the guest room as his parents continued to argue against her leaving.

"Do you have another set of sheets for the bed?" Cassie asked.

"I have no idea."

"You have no idea?"

"People come. They stay. They go. I strip the bed and wash the sheets and put them back on."

"Do you have a linen closet?"

They found another set of sheets and changed the linens, plus the bathroom towels. Cassie packed up, then set her belongings by the bedroom door.

They'd barely spoken.

"We'll stay in touch," she said.

"I can't believe you're leaving me here to eat cardboard."

She laughed. "I'm sure it's not that bad. Anyway, there's plenty of food in the refrigerator that will satisfy the carnivore in you."

"She will have already thrown it out. She'll want me to do a purging, too."

"What's that?"

"You don't want to know." He was playing it up because it was making her laugh.

"You'll survive," she said.

"Will you stop by now and then?"

"Sure. Keep me up-to-date on everything you hear from your lawyer, okay?"

"I will."

She turned away. He reached for her hand, stopping her. "Thank you for everything, especially getting me out of the house tonight."

"You're welcome."

He tried to see below the surface. She had a slight smile on her mouth, but not in her eyes. He lifted his other hand to cup her cheek. She didn't pull away, but she didn't lean into him, either. "You sleep with the light on."

"Yes."

"Why?"

"I don't want to talk about it."

She would've gone headstrong into the yard, barefoot and in pajamas, with a gun in her hand, but she had to have a light on when she slept? Her complexity intrigued him. "Stay," he repeated.

"I can't."

"You don't want to get to know my parents?"

He'd hit a nerve. Her eyes flickered with something. What? And why?

"I'm sure your parents are wonderful. It's obvious you don't just tolerate them."

Yes, he loved them, but they couldn't have picked a worse time for a surprise visit. He and Cassie were just getting to know each other.

"At least stay until morning. It's too late to be driving now."

"I pull all-night surveillances, Heath. This is no big deal."

"Cassie." He brushed his thumb along her cheek, then lifted his other hand to frame her face.

"Earthie," she responded.

He figured she was putting distance between them. They'd talked around their feelings before, both of them afraid to move too fast. He wasn't going to let her take too many steps away from what they'd begun. "Is Cassie short for Cassandra?"

"No."

"Short for anything?"

"I think 'any' or 'thing' would be short for anything."

He smiled. She clasped his wrists but didn't make him take his hands away from her face. She looked worried, though. Or scared. Of him? Of her feelings?

"We've been up here a long time. Your parents—"

He stopped her words with a kiss, more than a brush of lips, less than a merging. Her fingers tightened on his wrists, then drifted down to his waist. He tipped her head back a little, changed the angle of the kiss, took it deeper. Her lips parted on a sigh. Her arms wound around him. She pulled herself closer, aligning their hips. He moved her against the wall and pressed into her. Her breath caught, then she moaned. He slipped his tongue into her mouth, her warm, wet, welcoming mouth, and she lifted her body into his. He lost all sense of time. He only knew he wished he had forever.

She broke away, pressed her face into his shoulder. He gathered her close, felt her shake, heard her breathing slow. He waited for her to say something about it being a mistake, that they had said they would wait until everything was resolved before they saw where the relationship might go. He wasn't sorry. Nor did he want her to have regrets.

"Okay," she said at last. "Okay."

"Okay, what?" The kiss was just okay? Everything was okay?

She stepped away and picked up her overnight case, garment bag and briefcase.

"Okay, what?" he repeated.

"Now we know."

"Know what?"

"What's between us."

"You had doubts?" He'd been sure of his attraction. He thought she'd been, too.

"There's a difference between anticipation and actuality."

"So, the actuality matched the anticipation?"

"Surpassed it."

"And that scares you, Cassie? Worries you?"

She nodded.

"Because?"

"Earthie!" His mother's voice broke the tension, puncturing the cloud of privacy they'd made.

"I have to go," Cassie said, walking away at her usual fast clip.

"We'll talk about this."

She looked over her shoulder at him but didn't respond.

He didn't follow her to her car, but veered into the nursery, where his father was rocking a sleeping Danny while his mother rearranged the stacks of tiny clothing in a nearby dresser.

"Cassie said goodbye," he said, stepping into the room. *Goodbye.*

Cassie made an effort not to speed through the streets of Sausalito, forcing herself to pay attention to the road. Still her thoughts darted back to Heath and the kiss. She had learned as a child to compartmentalize her emotions, and in her career she hadn't been put in any dangerous situations yet that would test her ability to control her feelings. Risky, yes, but nothing life-threatening. Still she'd kept her head just fine—until now.

She'd known Heath was going to kiss her and had let him, even though she knew she shouldn't. What did that say about her? How could he break through years of self-discipline, and even more years of presenting an unemotional front, when she'd known him only four days?

She could've stopped him with a word. Instead she welcomed him, encouraged him, and even sought more.

Why?

Even if she knew why, did she want to acknowledge

it? She was scared—and a little desperate. Scared, she could live with. Scared, she understood. But, desperate? She couldn't remember feeling desperate before. She'd learned early to have a plan and follow it, which tended to eliminate the possibility of desperation.

But she hadn't counted on Heath. Or Danny.

She'd already laid claim to both of them. Foolish thing to do. Incredibly foolish thing to do. She should know better.

Cassie knew what would happen next. Heath's parents would stay long enough that everything with Danny would be settled—custody, a nanny, even Heath's comfort level as a new parent. He would be driving again, taking Danny places. His world would expand—without her.

Cassie wouldn't be necessary any longer. Once again, not necessary to anyone.

She paid the toll on the Golden Gate then headed for home. After a few minutes she punched the speed dial for Jamey on her cell phone.

"I know it's late—okay, really late—but could I come over?" she said when he answered.

"Sure. What's going on?"

"I'll tell you when I see you."

Jamey lived less than a mile from Cassie, but while she rented a studio apartment, he'd bought a house for the first time in his life, having given up a twenty-year career as a bounty hunter to finally settle down.

"You look like you just lost your best friend," he said to her when he invited her inside.

Okay, so maybe she wasn't so good at keeping her

feelings compartmentalized, after all—or at keeping her expression composed.

"Beer?" he asked when she said nothing.

"Thanks."

"Have a seat. I'll be right back."

She sat on the sofa, leaving the overstuffed chair for Jamey, but after a few seconds she pushed herself off the couch and paced the length of the room. Jamey passed her a bottle. She didn't sit down. He did. Then he waited.

"I'm not being objective," she said at last.

"About?"

"Heath."

"Ah."

She shared what happened—except for the kiss.

"Why did you leave?" he asked.

"Because he didn't need me there."

"Sounds like he did. He asked you to stay."

Cassie finally sat down. She took a long sip then leaned back, forcing her muscles to relax. "I don't want to get to know his parents."

"Why?"

"It just pulls me closer and closer, and…" She shrugged.

"It makes for another opportunity to get hurt."

"Yeah," she whispered. And Eva could come back, changing everything, as well.

"Too many people have come and gone in your life already. Too few have stayed."

She nodded. It was a painful admission. She had a hard time keeping people in her life, because she always tried to beat them to the punch and leave first.

"And your biological clock is ticking."

"That clock has been striking midnight since I was about thirteen years old."

"Is that part of the allure of Heath, do you think? He comes with a ready-made family?"

"Probably. But not completely. When he kissed—" She stopped.

"Ah."

"I thought I might not see him again," she muttered.

He laughed. "You don't do excuses well, Cass. A spade's a spade with you. Don't start now."

"Okay." She scraped the label on her bottle with her fingernail, avoiding Jamey's gaze. "He appeals to me. But you know what it's like being a P.I. It seems like an exotic job, so getting dates is easy. Building a relationship is hard."

"Can't blame it all on the profession, although I agree with you for the most part. Anyone who doesn't do nine-to-five has a tough time being a partner. But some of your problem in relationships has to do with your past. Your abandonment issues, if you want to get psychological about it, and your fear of caring too much, because it means you would have more to lose."

"I know. But knowing it doesn't seem to fix it. I have a social life. I have friends."

"And people are fascinated by what you do. At parties you're expected to entertain with tales of your derring-do."

"The problem is, we can't talk about our derring-do," she said.

"Right. Being a P.I. opens some doors, because people are fascinated, but closes others, for whatever reasons. We never know who to trust, do we, never know whether someone is interested in us or our jobs. I've been burned, too."

"But you have stories to tell from your past, Jamey. Scars. I was a paper pusher until I came to work at ARC. A researcher."

"And it's easy to be objective when you're dealing with facts. But this time you're dealing with a man and a baby. Give yourself a break, Cass. Relax. Do your job and see what happens from there."

She knew he was right, but it didn't stop her from wishing she hadn't left Heath's house, even as she also knew she'd done the right thing, professionally, by leaving. "This is too much for my puny mind. Talk to me about something else."

"My child turns eighteen this month."

She met his gaze. "You're getting anxious."

He nodded.

Cassie raised her bottle to him. "To the possibilities."

"The possibilities."

She stayed a little longer then made her way home. The daisies she'd bought on Friday brought a smile as she put away her clothes. She opened the sleeper sofa, straightened the bedding, then stacked pillows so that she could watch television for a few minutes in bed. Too late for Letterman, she settled on headline news. She picked up a piece of wood from her end table, a carved turtle, and ran her fingers over the surface. It wasn't smooth and polished, but primitive—and yet exquisite. At least to her.

She tucked it under her chin and pictured her grandfather sitting on the front stoop of his run-down old house, carving the turtle with the knife he sharpened with a whetstone. She could still hear the raspy sound of the blade across the stone. She could see him test the blade against his thumb, smell the scent of the wood as he whittled and carved, all the while talking to her about his past, the lessons learned, her mother.

Cassie had a box of small wooden carvings, her grandfather's and hers. Pieces of her past, her way of staying sane and keeping memories alive when there was no one else to share that part of her life with. No blood relative that she knew of. No best friend for life because she'd moved so much.

She wanted a family. She wanted ties that bound. Because of that she knew she was vulnerable to Heath and Danny in a way she never had been before.

Now she just had to figure out what to do about it.

Ten

Heath walked to the top of the driveway and eyed the long, bumpy road, now cleared of brush. Danny slept in his arms, having fallen asleep during their fifteen-minute walk around the property. Four men with chainsaws had spent the better part of the day getting rid of the overgrowth and hauling it away. The silence now soothed Heath, especially since his talkative mother was gone, too.

Which sounded harsh, he realized, when he'd actually enjoyed her more this time than ever before. He'd appreciated her spirit, her zest for life, her dive-right-in attitude. And his father had spoken up more. He and Heath had taken walks around the property, identifying what should be trimmed. He'd forgotten how much his father knew about such things.

But now Heath was waiting for Cassie. Although she'd come twice to visit during the week his parents had been there, he hadn't spoken to her alone, although he'd tried and she'd resisted, kindly but firmly. He'd started to push her a little until he saw something in her eyes that made him stop. She seemed nervous—or scared, he wasn't sure which.

So he made up reasons to call her at work, and she kept each conversation short and businesslike, except for a softening in her voice when she asked about Danny. And while she'd been sociable to his parents, she'd been aloof, too.

Or maybe just self-protective.

A complicated woman, Cassie Miranda. He'd caught her once—just once—watching him with what could only be called lust in her eyes. He'd just made a wish and blown out his birthday candles at an impromptu fortieth birthday party his parents put together. He'd looked at her, the object of his wish, and she'd looked back, as if his parents weren't there. As if they were a normal man and woman with normal attraction. Dream on.

He'd called her as soon as his parents announced they were leaving, hoping he wouldn't have to go over her head again to get her to return to…him. The job. But she'd said she would be back after work that evening, with no hesitation at all.

Heath turned to go back into his house when he heard a car heading up the driveway. Cassie. Adrenaline rushed through him, jump-starting his heart, his lungs, his muscles, and everything else that mattered.

Danny stirred as Heath went to meet her at the car.

"You got your forest tamed," she said, after reaching for her briefcase.

She smelled good. Not like perfume but something totally unique. Maybe just her shampoo. Whatever it was, he wished he could wallow in it. "It's just the beginning," he said calmly, as if he didn't want to sweep her into his arms and kiss the daylights out of her. "The crew will be back later to finish the rest of the property."

"That's great. How's my Danny Boy?" she asked, bending over him and giving him a kiss. He turned his head toward her. Heath almost did the same.

"He survived his first week of Grammy Crystal."

Cassie grinned. "And you?"

"I need meat."

"Groceries are in the trunk."

He passed Danny to her, not trying to avoid touching her as he had in the past. He wanted to touch. Needed to. She kept her focus on the baby, not giving Heath a hint about her feelings, but he didn't believe it was just a job to her anymore.

As he got the food and her belongings out of the car he watched her walk toward the house, her face close to Danny's as she whispered to him. They met up in the kitchen, where he set down her suitcase and garment bag so that he could put away the groceries.

"How's he been sleeping? Any pattern emerging?" Cassie asked.

"He likes Letterman," Heath said.

"Yeah? Me, too. I'll take that shift. Otherwise, what does he do?"

"He's been taking a bottle every three hours, pretty regularly. As for sleep—you never know. The last couple of days he's had a crying jag between four and seven in the evening." He glanced at his watch. A half hour to go. "Nothing seems to help. Even Mom couldn't get him to stop."

"Do you put him in his crib and let him cry or do you hold him?"

"Both. It's all guesswork, still. Are we having steak for dinner?"

She nodded. "And salad and baked potatoes."

"Thank you for coming back."

"You were that desperate for steak?"

He didn't know what to make of the distance she was keeping, physically and with her choice of words. For her to joke after he thanked her—well, it wasn't like her.

She shifted Danny into a new position, so that his head was tucked between her shoulder and neck. He looked so tiny that way, curled into her.

"Why are you avoiding looking at me?" he asked.

She closed her eyes briefly, then got up from the bar stool and walked to a window. The blinds were raised, as they had been since the first time she'd opened them more than a week ago.

"I don't trust myself," she said after a minute.

"With me?"

She nodded. He came up behind her, not touching her, but the proximity alone arousing him.

He asked the question that had been on his mind all week. "How much of it is me, and how much is Danny?"

"You're a package."

"You can't separate it out?"

"Do you mean would I be attracted to you without Danny?"

"Yeah."

"We wouldn't have met without Danny."

"That's not an answer."

"Heath," she said, a smile in her voice, "I think between us we have enough issues to keep a psychologist on retainer full-time."

He agreed. "All right, Cassie. We won't talk about it."

"How did your interview with the woman from the nanny agency go?" she asked.

"Fine." He hadn't told the woman to send candidates. He wasn't ready. Not to have a nanny there, and not to give up Cassie.

She turned around, a slight smile on her face. He couldn't do it, couldn't not touch her, not kiss her. Maybe it was better that they get this out of the way. If she felt she couldn't stay, so be it. He wouldn't force her.

"Cassie."

Her brows lifted.

He cupped her face. He felt her pull Danny a little closer to her.

"What are you doing?" she asked.

He kissed her, not hard, not long, but enough to make the point that it was no simple greeting from friend to friend. Then just when she leaned into him he backed off. He had his answer. "I missed you," he said.

She swallowed. "I missed you, too."

The phone rang. The caller ID said Private Party, which he usually let go to the answering machine, but he grabbed it and said hello, his mood upbeat. He brushed a hand over Danny's silky hair. Every day his world got a little better, a little brighter.

"Heath?"

The voice was female and hesitant. "Eva?" He locked gazes with Cassie. "Where are you?"

"At a friend's house. I just wanted…I was wondering how the baby is."

"He's fine. He's beautiful. Do you—" he forced the words "—want to see him?"

"No. I— No."

"Where are you living? How can I get in touch with you?"

"Heath…"

"What?"

Silence. Heath waited for as long as he could stand it.

"Are you sure you want to give him up, Eva?"

"I'm sure."

She hung up before he could coax an address out of her, but not before he heard the hitch in her voice. He cradled the receiver, left his hand on it.

"You are a good man," Cassie said.

"What makes you say that?"

"You asked if she was sure."

"Some people would argue that I was just looking out for my own interests."

"Some people didn't see your face. Didn't see you look at Danny. Didn't know what it would cost you to give him up, even part-time."

He shrugged. He didn't want a medal, just a chance to be a father again. A more involved one. One Danny could count on to keep him safe. Forever.

Cassie stepped into the shower late that night and closed her eyes. Exhaustion settled in her bones. She'd sent Heath to his office to work while Danny cried his little heart out for his four o'clock to seven o'clock cry time. Even *itsy bitsy spider* hadn't helped, sung quietly in his room with his door shut.

She'd read baby-care books while she rocked and walked him, and decided he had colic. He finally took a bottle and fell asleep, worn-out. When he woke up he was his placid self again, undemanding and content while they had dinner. Heath had headed to his office again after dinner, prodded by Cassie, who did some work herself, until it was time to feed Danny again.

When she realized she was falling asleep standing up in the shower, she turned off the water and stepped out. A few minutes later she folded down the quilt. She found an envelope with her name on it. Inside was a short note:

Dear Cassie,
It was wonderful meeting you. Thank you for making our son laugh again. And remember, you only regret what you don't do. Peace, Crystal and Journey.

What did they mean by that thing about regret? she wondered, even as she smiled at the note itself. She'd found them to be down-to-earth, fun and warm. Yes, she could see Heath's point—his mother talked a lot. But she told great stories and wasn't mean-spirited or gossipy. If things were different… Well, she was glad she hadn't spent more time with them than she had. She'd liked them both.

Cassie climbed into bed just as Danny's cry came over the intercom. She heard Heath walk down the hall and decided to stay in bed. She would get Danny the next time.

She was almost asleep when there was a knock on her door. "Cassie?"

She sat up. "What?"

"Danny and I want to know if you'd like to watch Letterman with us."

She stifled a yawn. "Sure. Give me a minute."

"We'll be in my bedroom."

He padded across to his room. Cassie sat staring at the opposite wall. In his bedroom? O-kay.

She'd remembered to bring a robe this time, so she put it on before crossing the hall. He was propped against his headboard with his knees raised, Danny nestled along his thighs. She looked for a chair to drag close to the bed. The only chair in the room was an over-stuffed lounge chair, far too big to move.

"We won't bite," he said, patting the bed beside him, his eyes on the television as the Letterman theme song started.

I might bite you, though, she thought with a smile. How he tempted her, tormented her. The way he'd kissed her that afternoon when she thought she'd been warning him off…she had to admit she liked it. Liked the way he took charge. Now here she was in his bedroom, albeit with Danny, too, but *he* was no threat to her equilibrium.

She shoved a few pillows against the headboard then sat, stretching out her legs, drawing her robe tighter. It would be a testament to her self-control if she resisted inching closer. How long had it been since she'd cuddled up with someone to watch television? Had she ever? She must have, but she couldn't remember when.

As the monologue began, Cassie let Danny grab her finger and hold tight. He turned his head toward her when she spoke.

"Does he watch the whole show?" she asked.

"He likes the Top Ten list."

"Seriously?"

"I think it's the laughter. Maybe he's destined to be an actor."

They lay there on the king-size bed. She closed her eyes and listened to the monologue, smiling at the jokes, hearing Heath laugh occasionally. It felt good. Nice…

She woke up with a start. Panic gripped her. Darkness surrounded her. She clutched her robe

"Easy," she heard Heath say soothingly. "You're okay."

"No." She jackknifed up, started to scramble off the bed. She had to find light. She had to see.

"Cassie—"

"Turn on the light. Turn on the light."

He did. Light flared from his bedside lamp across the bed. She saw the questioning concern in his eyes. Sweat pulled her pajamas closer to her skin.

"Are you all right?" he asked.

She nodded. She was, now. "Sorry."

"What happened?"

She didn't want to talk about it with him. Not now. Not yet. It was embarrassing that a twenty-nine-year-old woman had to have the light on to sleep.

"I put Danny to bed," he said, filling up the silence. "I turned off the television. Then as soon as I turned off the light you woke up," he said.

She said nothing. After a minute he put his arms around her and drew her close. She held herself stiff, her arms tucked close to her chest as a barrier, not wanting to give in to his comfort.

"Rest," he said, his breath dusting her hair.

"Don't turn off the light."

"I won't."

She let herself relax, taking several minutes before she nestled against him, both of them still sitting up.

"You okay?" he asked.

"I should go to my room." But she didn't make a move to do so.

He tightened his hold. She liked the feel of his body, the scent of his skin and the warmth of him, top to bottom. She wanted to get closer, to lie down with him. She didn't dare to.

"You're afraid of the dark," he said.

She didn't respond.

"I'm afraid of falling asleep," he said. "I dream about my son. About Kyle. I hate falling asleep."

"I'm sorry."

"It's been better since you've been here."

"Since Danny," she corrected.

"Both of you."

She was too comfortable with him. She wanted too much to stay with him, to sleep in his arms. She couldn't. She could fall in love with him so easily, and he was just beginning to open up to the world. He had a lot of catching up to do. He couldn't be tied down again so soon.

And she had an ideal of a happy family, one that was probably impossible for her to attain. She would ruin things at some point. She always did.

But how could she ignore him when he rubbed her

back like that, the strokes long and even. Her eyes stung
and her throat burned.

"Want to lie down?" he asked.

"I need to go to my own bed," she said, pushing away.

He let her go. She didn't even say good-night but hurried across the hall. As soon as she reached her bedroom
she regretted leaving him, knowing she was giving him
mixed messages. She turned to go back, not sure what
she would say, and came face-to-face with him. She
hadn't heard him follow.

He moved a little closer to her, not crowding her but
not giving her a lot of space, either. "If you'd stayed in
my bed," he said, "I wouldn't have touched you unless
you wanted me to. You don't have to be afraid of me."

"I'm not afraid of you. I'm afraid of *me*. I don't trust
myself. I told you that earlier. Last week when you
kissed me—here, in this room—if your parents hadn't
been here…"

He framed her face with his hands, his touch gentle,
and then he kissed her, a long, searching, tender kiss that
made her eyes sting and her toes curl. She slid her arms
around him, giving in to the demand building inside her.
Without her wearing her boots he seemed so much
taller, which made her feel feminine, a rarity for her. She
wished she was wearing something silky and soft.

He moved his hands down her back, a long, slow
drag, ending at her hips, then pulled her against him. She
moaned at the feel of him, hard and tempting, pressed
into her abdomen. His mouth opened, his tongue sought
hers. She met it, welcomed it, welcomed him, as she
went up on tiptoe, winding her arms around his neck.
His lips were soft and firm, gentle and bold, cautious

and daring. A kiss for the memory book from this stealer of breath and heart.

"Come sleep with me," he murmured in her ear. "Just sleep."

"Too tempting." She hated to say it, hated being sensible and reasonable and mature, but she was looking out for him as much as herself. And yet she couldn't stop touching him, letting her fingers comb through his hair, drift down his neck. She wanted so much to give in to him, to the pleasure, to the joy.

He scooped her into his arms, drawing a shriek from her. "We're going to my room," he said. "Sleep in my bed. What happens after that is up to you."

He carried her across the hall and set her on his bed. After a minute she felt him touch her braid.

"I've never seen you with your hair down," he said. "May I?"

The question required more than an answer—it required a decision. Freeing her hair meant freeing her passion. She didn't doubt that for a minute. What should she do? Anything could happen between them. Should she give in to her need for him because it might be her only opportunity to do so? Or *not* give in to her need because it might be her only opportunity?

Make a memory or not? Now or never?

You only regret the things you don't do. The words from his parents' note to her came back. Whether or not she bought into the theory, she wanted to believe it was reason enough to make love with him tonight, with no regrets in the morning or the future.

She started to pull off the band from the end of the braid.

"I'll do it," he said quietly. "Please."

"Okay."

She felt him tug the band off her hair, then he unbraided it, slowly, carefully, until her hair lay across her back like a cape. She closed her eyes, enjoying his touch, his attention. She'd watched his hands cradle Danny, stroke his hair, pat his back. Now they worked magic on her instead, both hands tunneling through her hair like gentle combs.

"Beautiful," he said. "You're beautiful. I don't think you know that about yourself."

"No—"

"I thought it the first time I saw you."

She looked over her shoulder at him.

"And fierce," he added. "Protective. Kind. Brave. Nurturing. Scared."

"Scared?"

He nodded. "Of commitment. Of the disappointment that so often comes with it."

"You've learned all that about me in two and a half weeks?"

He sat up, lifted her hair over her shoulders, and massaged her back. "All that and more. My mother pointed something out, though, that made everything click."

"What was that?"

"That she'd never seen anyone work harder at keeping their distance than you. I started to pay attention then—to how you clench your fists when your eyes say you want to touch. To how you take a step back when the rest of your body seems to be leaning forward. You don't let yourself give in to what comes naturally. Except that you didn't try to keep your distance from Danny."

He'd summed her up. There was no defense. "No."
*And I'm not keeping my distance from you, even though
I should. But, no regrets.*

"Heath?"

"Cassie?"

"I'm saying yes."

Eleven

She said yes.

Heath didn't know if he'd made the wisest or stupidest decision of his life by bringing her into his room, but there was no turning back now. He wanted her with a depth of passion he hadn't known in a very long time.

Everything about her appealed to him in some base way, whether in sex appeal, maternal instinct or job efficiency. A complete package. He knelt beside her on the bed then was surprised to find his hands shaking when he touched her face.

"I'm glad," she said softly, making eye contact.

"About what?"

She wrapped her hands around his. "That you're as excited as I am. My heart is thundering so much I can hardly hear anything."

"You are the sexiest woman I've ever known," he said.

"What?"

"You are the—" He stopped when her eyes sparkled at her joke, then the sparkle turned to brilliance as she slid her hands down his chest, stopping at his waistband. She slipped a hand under his T-shirt and touched skin. He sucked in a breath as her fingernails scraped his flesh.

"I take it you're not sleepy," he said.

"My little nap was enough to keep me awake for hours."

"Hours?"

"Can't rise to the occasion?" She smiled seductively.

He didn't know what to make of the playful Cassie, except to enjoy her.

"You've already gotten a rise out of me," he said, untying the sash of her robe.

"I noticed."

"Are you on the Pill?" he asked as she slipped out of her robe and tossed it aside.

"Yes."

He knew she wouldn't lie to him. She was well aware of what Eva had done, and Cassie wouldn't do the same. "Anything else I should know?"

She shook her head. "You?"

"No."

"Twenty-first century reality sure pours ice water on romance, doesn't it?" she asked, suddenly looking hesitant.

Time to change the tone. Time to let her know how much he wanted her. He peeled his T-shirt over his head and dropped it. Before he could reach for her, she leaned close and kissed his chest.

"Do you have any idea how long I've wanted to do

that?" she asked, her tongue making swirls, leaving cool, damp trails that chilled and excited, teased and tormented.

"Not as long as I've wanted to do the same to you," he said, moving her back, stopping her. He liked her assertiveness, liked that she wasn't afraid to show she wanted him. But his control was going to last about half a minute if she kept doing that. "Let me show you," he said.

She sat quietly as he unbuttoned her top and pushed it over her shoulders. He whispered her name as her breasts were bared, then resisted the temptation to touch, making her wait, making her want. He grabbed the waistband of her bottoms and tugged them down and off.

"Exquisite," he said as he slid his bottoms off, too. "Perfect."

She dragged her hands down his chest, wrapped her fingers around him, her fingertips like fire. "Not sure that's a good idea," he said, struggling against the need threatening to burst.

"I need to touch you."

He moved her hands, held them by the wrists and sat back on his heels. "Later."

Her body was amazing—lean and muscled, yet curved and soft. He kissed her hard, unable to keep things slow a second longer. Her tongue met his thrust for thrust as he pressed her into the mattress and stretched out on top of her. Her legs opened, welcoming him, but he wanted more first. More of her mouth. More of her breasts. The taste of her nipples, hot and hard. The feel of her skin, damp and smooth. The temptation of the sublime femaleness of her body as he moved down her, savoring and appreciating and arousing. She arched high, moaned low, begged softly. He dragged his fingers up her thigh, stopping at the apex to stroke her lightly, learning her, appreciating her, going deeper with each touch.

"I can't," she said. "I—"

"Can't what?"

"Wait. Wait. I can't—"

"Then don't wait."

"Together," she said, the word gritty. "I want it to be together."

"In a minute." He caressed her, teased her, found the places that made her gasp, settled his mouth there.

She grabbed hold of his hair as if to stop him even as she tipped her pelvis toward him, then she exploded with sound and motion, pleasing him, exciting him. Before she could come down, he moved up her body and drove into her, her welcome tight and hot. He'd barely begun to move when she came again, louder, more violently, the sounds dragging on and on, her legs wrapping tighter around him. Then he was lost, too, in the pleasure, in the heat, in the beauty, in the wonder. *There's no place like home.* He wanted it to last forever, be forever, take forever....

When reality touched him again and he was spent, he lay sprawled on her, not wanting to give up possession. "Can you breathe?" he asked after a while.

Silence.

"Cassie?"

Still nothing.

He pulled back. She drew a long, sucking, gasping breath that turned into a laugh.

"Brat," he said then he dropped onto his side, leaving a hand on her abdomen.

Her smile was so tender and sweet he almost couldn't associate it with her. Another fascinating side of the complex Ms. Miranda.

"Was it good for you?" he asked, hiding his grin.

She shoved him.

"Is that a yes?"

"You know it was," she countered.

"Yeah, I heard it loud and clear."

Her cheeks pinkened. He was amazed. Tough girl Cassie was embarrassed that she enjoyed sex in a way no one could doubt.

"Stay with me," he said seriously. "Sleep with me."

"You're just looking to get lucky again."

No, he wasn't. But he would play along with her. "What if I am?"

"Then I'll definitely stay." She laid a hand along his face. "Can you sleep with the light on?"

"Anything you need."

Her eyes took on a little sheen. She raised up enough to kiss him, then he gathered the blankets around them and pulled her close. When he felt her relax he said, "Why are you afraid of the dark?"

"I don't want to talk about it."

"Why not?"

"Because it sounds stupid."

"Fears often are, but that doesn't make them any less real."

She didn't respond. After a few minutes he closed his eyes.

"My angel can't find me in the dark," she said quietly.

He tucked her closer. "Tell me about your angel."

"When I first was sent to my grandfather after my mother died, I couldn't sleep at night. My mother died during the night, and I guess I figured my grandfather might, too, if I fell asleep. Who knows what goes through the mind of a five-year-old? Anyway, he put a night-light in my room so that my angel—the one specifically assigned to me—could find me and kiss me good-night, then I could sleep."

Her voice had gotten small, as if she was five again. He pressed his lips to her head.

"You're the first person I've told. I've never spent the night with anyone before, because I didn't want them to know."

"Thank you for your faith in me."

She shifted a little, not moving away from him, but seeming to get closer. She slipped a leg between his. "When he died, when I was nine, I took the night-light with me to my foster home. The kids I shared the room with complained that they couldn't sleep. They took the night-light away. I screamed and cried and begged. Finally they let me sleep in the bathtub so I could keep the night-light in there with me. They got rid of me pretty fast."

A hundred curses ran through his mind. She was just a little girl. A child who had lost her mother, an addict who probably hadn't been the greatest mother in the world to begin with, but the only one Cassie knew, then she'd lost her grandfather, who sounded like a hell of a guy.

"Of course, I had a knife, too, that I wouldn't give up," she said, changing the tone.

"What kind of knife?"

"A good one. Grandpa whittled and carved. He taught me. It was the only thing of his I kept when he died, that and some of his carvings. They took the knife away, but I found it and hid it. After that I made sure no one knew I had it, although the social workers speculated in their reports that I still did. They just didn't know how stealthy I could be." She smiled. "You probably think I'm crazy."

"I think you're brave." No wonder she championed children.

"Just a survivor."

"Much more than that."

She yawned and nestled. "I'm tired."

"Sleep," he said softly. "Your angel will come."

He felt her smile against his chest.

"Thank you, Gabriel."

A minute later she was asleep. He thought about the life she'd lived. Thought about how quickly she'd loved Danny and how she was probably going to have to give him up, another loss among many. Thought about Kyle and his short, sweet life. How he would be alive today if not for Heath's ego and arrogance.

Danny's I'm-hungry cry came over the monitor. Cassie didn't budge when he slipped out of the bed and hurried to shut it off before it woke her. He found his pajamas and T-shirt in opposite corners of the room, then started out the door.

"I'm coming, too," she said, sitting up, still naked, looking bewildered, and sexy as hell.

"Sleep, Cassie. You can take the next turn."

She got out of bed, gathered her pajamas. "I'm coming," she repeated, coming up beside him.

He closed his eyes and nodded, then he waited for her to dress. Together they held hands and went to take care of their baby.

Twelve

Today's the day, Heath thought—the first day of the rest of his life. Cliché or not, it was the truth. The gardeners were finished cleaning up the property, leaving the view wide-open, as he'd intended when he built the house. His car had just been returned from the mechanic, who had cleaned the fuel system, changed the oil and got it into running condition again. It sat in front of the garage, ready to take Cassie and Danny for a drive when she got home from work, which would be soon.

She'd been living there for a week, had spent every night in his bed, in his arms. Laughter and light filled the house finally.

He'd made a decision about who to name as Danny's guardian. He'd called Kerwin and left a message for him so that they could start the paperwork.

He was in a great mood.

He still hadn't opened the blinds in his office—another big step to take sometime in the future. Having Danny didn't resolve every issue, but he had turned Heath's life around.

Then there was Cassie. Elusive, complicated, sexy Cassie, a mother and a lover, a rescuer of babies and lost souls. There was so much more he wanted to know about her.

He heard her car coming up the driveway and went out to greet her. She parked next to his car.

"Going somewhere?" she asked.

"I thought we would."

She smiled. "Around the world in eighty days?"

"Around the town in sixty minutes, maybe? Won't know until we get there."

"Sounds good to me. How's Danny?"

"It's five-thirty and he isn't crying."

"Progress."

They walked side by side. He took her hand. "I have a question for you," he said.

"Sounds serious."

"My lawyer reminded me that I need to appoint a legal guardian for Danny should something happen to me. I want that person to be you."

She stopped walking to stare at him. "Your parents…"

"They will always be his grandparents. That may be the worst of it for you." He smiled. She didn't. "You love him. That's what matters. Not blood."

Her eyes welled. She put her arms around him. "I've never been more honored. Thank you."

The phone rang. "That's probably Kerwin. I left a message for him to call."

He hurried into the house, picking up the phone right before the answering machine would've come on.

"Heath, it's Kerwin."

"Thanks for returning my call. You got my message?"

"Yes, I—"

"I just asked her." Cassie shut the front door and crossed the foyer. "She's agreed to be guardian."

"I don't know how to tell you this," Kerwin said.

"Tell me what?"

A few beats passed. Cassie tiptoed into Danny's room.

"The DNA results are in. Heath, you're not Daniel's father."

"We're going for a drive," Cassie said to Danny as she changed his diaper. She'd found him awake in his crib, his little arms and legs in motion. He'd kicked off his blanket. "We'll celebrate this momentous occasion in your life. It's kind of momentous for your daddy, too, you know, driving again."

She didn't hear Heath approach, but suddenly he was there.

"His cord fell off," Cassie said, lifting Danny's shirt to show him the cute little belly button. "Look. He's got an innie— What's wrong?"

His expression bleak, Heath stared at Danny. "He's not mine," he said.

"What?"

"The DNA came back. I'm not his father."

Cassie's feet turned to lead. Her stomach churned. Her heart stopped. She couldn't move, not even to hug him. She kept a hand on Danny's stomach, her throat convulsing. She'd known. She'd suspected all along that Eva had been lying to Heath. Her story hadn't rung true. But Cassie had chosen lately to ignore the possibilities because she'd fallen hard for Danny—and his father. It wasn't like her to ignore reality.

"Heath—"

"Don't say anything," he said, then walked out of the room.

Seconds later, she heard his office door shut quietly. Too quietly. She would've preferred he slammed it or banged a fist through it.

She was partly to blame. She'd encouraged him to give his heart to Danny and not worry about the future. If he'd held back—

No. He wouldn't have held back. He'd loved Danny before he was born, even though he'd been afraid to.

She picked up the boy and cuddled him close. She'd known it was too good to be true. A man to love? A baby to love? It wasn't in the cards for her. The one time she'd let herself believe it might be possible…

Cassie shifted Danny so that she could see his face, his sweet, sweet face. So helpless. And such a pawn in Eva's game, whatever it was. That kind of cruelty could never be forgiven. Why *had* Eva left her baby with Heath? Cassie could only speculate. Danny would recover, although his life wouldn't be as rich by not having Heath as his father. But what about Heath? Would he recover?

Would *she?* She couldn't afford to think about it right now. Whatever emotions were simmering needed to stay simmering. Danny needed her now more than ever.

She wrapped him in a blanket and went outdoors. They walked all around the property, enjoying the sun and the view, until he let her know he was hungry. She fed him and rocked him to sleep, then put him in his bassinet, her hands lingering on him as she pulled the blanket up to his chin. She bent over and kissed him. "Night-night, sweet pea." A sob rose from her chest. She pressed her hand to her mouth and whirled away, running from the room.

She stood at the bottom of the staircase until she felt steady enough to approach Heath. Then she started up. Not trying to be quiet, she made her way to his office door and knocked. After a few seconds he opened it.

"I don't want sympathy," he said, his face lined with pain.

She understood his need to hold himself together. She was being held together only with the glue of determination. "Okay. But we need to talk about what to do next."

"Yeah." His body rigid, he walked away then took a seat at his desk.

She sat, as well. "Aside from the test results, what did your lawyer tell you?"

"That I have to turn Dan—the baby over to Child Protective Services."

"No, you don't."

"Why not?"

"Because I know the system, and I can work around the system. If you don't want to turn him over, you don't have to. Not until Eva is found. Or his...someone else with legal authority to take him."

"I don't understand."

"Eva willingly left him with you. That counts. You're providing a good home. He's being well taken care of. And, Heath, I won't put him with CPS, period. If you don't want him, I'll take him."

"You say that like you'd be able to keep him forever."

"I won't. I know I won't. But I'll gladly keep him until the right person claims him."

He scrubbed his face with his hands. "Why did she do it, Cassie?"

She melted at the pain in his words. "She liked you."

"What?"

"She chose you. She seduced you, didn't she? You haven't said so, but I'll bet it's true."

He nodded.

"Heath, we know now that someone else fathered the baby, but she must've already known she was pregnant when you slept with her, because you thought she had three weeks to go before she would give birth. She knew she didn't. Apparently she doesn't want the real father to know."

"But she's smart enough to figure out I would do DNA tests."

"And she counted on the fact you would do exactly what you did—love him and fight for him."

"Can I? Fight for him?"

"I don't know. But you don't have to give him up just yet, unless you want to. Do you want to?"

He was silent for a very long time. She studied his profile—his long, shiny hair, his strong jaw and sharp cheekbones, the straight line of his nose. His beautiful hands, clenching and unclenching. "It would be like being a foster parent, wouldn't it?" he asked, facing her. "Take him in until the right home is found. Love him. Let him go."

"Yes."

"I don't want anyone else to have him."

"I know. Me, neither."

"I thought she would come and take him back. I never expected this."

"What do you want to do?" She kept after him, staying on task as much as possible. If she didn't she was going to break down like she never had before. Danny... My baby. My heart. My love.

"What would we have to do?"

She straightened her shoulders, getting down to business. "I make a call to Missing Persons first, see if anyone reported Eva missing, then see who did. It might lead to something. Then I'll go over to CPS and talk to them. We need to make it all legal, if there's any chance at all of making it permanent."

"Someone will want him," he said. "Someone else gave him life and will want him."

"You don't know that. Can you do it? Can you continue to keep him?"

"Without question."

That's what she wanted to hear—conviction.

"And still give him up?"

"I won't have a choice, will I?"

"Then I'll get busy. I can't go to CPS until they open again in the morning, but I'll call my contact at Missing Persons."

"Do it now. Here."

"Okay. He'll be off duty, but he'll remember the

name, if she's on the list. I've got to get my address book from my briefcase. I'll be right back."

She needed a couple of minutes away from him, away from his sorrow that threatened to expose hers. He probably thought she didn't care as much as he did. Maybe it was a good thing if he thought that. It would make the break easier in the end, not only from Danny but from Heath. He wouldn't want her around if Danny was gone. He already had to live with the pain of losing Kyle, and that would never go away. The pain of losing Danny would lessen in time, but not if she was there as a reminder every day.

Cassie splashed cold water on her face before she got her address book and returned to the office. She caught him staring into space, looking so alone. She wanted to wrap her arms around him and never let go. She knocked on the open door instead and walked in.

She didn't say a word, just headed to the phone and dialed.

"Speak," came the voice from the other end.

"Hey, Johnson, it's Cassie Miranda. How're you?"

"Cassie, my angel, my one and only. I'm good, babe. How're you doing?"

"Working hard."

"When don't you?"

"Hey, I'm on a case that might be linked to something you've got. Maybe. I'm wondering if you've got an MP for an Eva Brooks."

"Brooks. Nope. Not officially, anyway."

"What do you mean?"

"You're the second person to inquire about her recently."

"Who else was asking?"

Heath came to attention.

"Some lawyer," Johnson said.

"Kerwin Rudyard?"

"No. Let me think. Who the hell was that? Oh, yeah. Torrance. Brad Torrance."

Heath's corporate attorney and Eva's boss. He'd called her roommate, Darcy, too. "Okay, thanks. Listen, give me a buzz if anyone files a report, okay? I'd appreciate it."

"Sure thing. Take it easy."

"You, too." She hung up the phone. "Brad Torrance made an inquiry."

"Torrance? You find that odd, I take it."

"Yes and no. She dropped out of sight. Maybe the company wanted to talk to her about something, a paycheck perhaps, or her maternity benefits, but wouldn't it be the human resources director? Not the boss, I don't think."

They stared at each other.

"What do you know about him?" she asked.

"He's married. His wife is expecting a baby, as a matter of fact. She was due the same time as Eva. But I don't socialize with him, so I don't know more than that."

"How do you know she was pregnant?"

"Eva told me."

"How did it come up in conversation?"

He thought about it. "I think she said something about Torrance's wife coming into the office one day and, I don't know, they compared bellies, or something like that. What are you thinking? That he's the father? That they had an affair?"

"Makes sense, doesn't it? Eva was insistent, you said, that she couldn't tell anyone at work who the father was. Maybe it had nothing to do with it being a client, you, but with it being the boss," she said, warming to the idea even more.

"The boss would try to keep it hush-hush, anyway, of course, but especially with his wife pregnant," he said. "I think I should call him."

She thought about it. "Yeah, probably. But not tonight, not at home. Tomorrow at work. You'll have to be circumspect."

"I've been that since I was a day old. I've never forgiven my parents, either."

"Okay—" She stopped. Saw a twinkle in his eye. If he could joke at a time like this, she didn't need to worry about him. He would recover. "Wise guy."

Danny started to cry. The sound drifted up the staircase and into the office like butterflies, elusive and fragile. She looked at Heath, who had shut his eyes. After a few seconds he stood.

"I'll get him," he said.

She squeezed his arm as he passed by. He stopped for a second, his soul in his eyes, then kept walking. She waited where she was, giving him time alone, then made her way to the kitchen to make a dinner that neither of them would feel like eating.

They could pretend for one more night that he was theirs.

Heath wasn't sure he wanted Cassie to join him in bed. He didn't know what to do. He didn't want to talk. He didn't want to make love. He couldn't grieve. To grieve for Danny meant it opened the door for Kyle. He wasn't ready to face that, not now. Not yet.

Letterman was on but Danny, off his normal schedule all evening, was already asleep. Cassie was doing whatever she was doing. He didn't know.

After a few minutes she tapped lightly on his door. "Hi," she said, peeking in first, then coming into the room. Bathed in the blue light of the television, she looked otherworldly, yet he knew she was as earthbound as a person could get.

She walked to the bed, climbed onto it and sat cross-legged, facing him. "I was lonely."

He didn't say anything. He knew it hurt her. He didn't know how to tell her what he wanted, and didn't want.

"Dance with me," he said, deciding spur of the moment. It would be something new, a distraction, not likely to lead to deep conversation.

Although she was obviously surprised, she said okay. He held her hand as they got out of bed. He turned off the television, picked up another remote control and music filled the room, something slow, a tune he didn't recognize. She came into his arms like she'd been born to. How long had it been since he'd danced? Years and years. He was glad he'd asked her.

"Do you do this often?" he asked against her hair.

"Not slow dance. I go to clubs with friends. Lots of no-name dancing."

Her breath tickled his neck. "No name?"

"Somebody asks you to dance. You do. End of story."

"You don't get dates that way?"

"No."

"You're not asked?"

"I don't say yes. Too risky."

"Anyone get pushy?"

"Nah. I show 'em my gun if they do. Amazing how fast they lose interest."

"You're kidding."

"Yes."

He heard the smile in her voice.

"This is nice, Heath."

Yes, it was nice. And arousing. He could feel her breasts press against his chest. He rested a hand against the small of her back, his thumb stroking her spine. There was the slightest change in her body, a tightening, a little move closer. She went up on tiptoe.

"I've never been able to understand how women can do that."

"What?"

"Dance on their toes."

"Makes it easier to follow."

"What do you do if the guy's shorter than you?"

"Lead."

He laughed when he thought himself incapable of laughter, whirled her around then dipped her backward. He let his lips brush hers before pulling her up and continuing the dance, but he slowed the pace until just their bodies were moving, not their feet. He wrapped both arms around her. She nestled her face against his neck.

After a minute he felt a drop of hot water land on his skin and slip under his T-shirt, then another, then another. He swallowed. *Ah, Cassie. I wish I could let you mourn. I can't. I can't.*

"Let's go to bed," he said, not even acknowledging her tears.

"I don't want—I'm not—"

"To sleep," he said. "Just to sleep."

"Okay." Her relief filled the room.

A barrier sat between them, even as they clung to each other in bed. No words were spoken. He knew she stayed awake for as long as he did—until Danny woke up.

The difference was, this time she let him go alone.

Thirteen

Cassie woke with a start, found the bed empty beside her, fired a glance at the clock and fell back against the pillow, stunned. Nine o'clock. How could she have slept that late?

She hurried across the hall, showered, dressed and jogged downstairs, braiding her hair as she went.

"In the kitchen," Heath called out.

He was at the stove, finishing up an omelet. Danny was kicking his legs, making his bouncy chair move on the counter near Heath.

"I overslept," she said, breathless after rushing.

"You were tired." He slid the omelet onto a plate, sprinkled some chopped chives over the top, added two pieces of bacon and set the plate on the counter, motioning her to sit. Then he came around to her side and kissed her.

"Good morning," he said, smiling, but with hesitance in his eyes.

Because her first reaction was to pull away, she put her hands on his face and kissed him back. She hadn't liked his mother's accurate assessment of her, that she worked hard at keeping her distance. "Good morning. Thank you for breakfast."

"You're welcome."

"How's our— How's Danny this morning?"

He cupped the back of her head in sympathy for her slip. "Content. He's about ready for a bottle and a nap."

She took a bite of the omelet and sighed at the wonderful mix of sharp cheddar cheese and green pepper filling. "Have you called Brad Torrance yet?"

"I figured he wouldn't be in before nine. I'll call when Danny's asleep and the house is quiet."

She'd awakened at one point during the night trying to come up with reasons why they could delay calling Torrance, but none came to her. If it were her child gone missing—

"I think we're on to something with him," she said.

"Makes sense. If it's true, I don't envy him telling his wife. I wonder if she's given birth yet."

She was aware they were both trying to keep their conversation light, so that they wouldn't dwell on the implications of their speculation.

A half hour later they couldn't delay any longer. Danny was asleep. They went to Heath's office. Cassie held a portable phone so that she could listen in on the call. While they waited to be connected with Torrance, Heath put a hand on Cassie's and squeezed it.

"It's going to be okay," he said.

No, it wasn't, but she smiled back at him.

"How are you, Heath?" Torrance asked when he came on the line.

"Pretty good. Yourself?"

"Busy, as always. You were on my mind this morning, actually. We haven't had any work from you for a few weeks."

"I've been busy, but not in need of any contracts. Pretty soon, though. I've got three projects in the works."

"Great. What can I do for you, then?"

Heath glanced at Cassie. "I was curious about Eva Brooks."

The pause was so brief, Cassie decided Torrance could've just as easily been distracted for a second. "What about her?"

"You know she used to come here once a week or so to drop off papers. I was wondering if she'd had her baby yet. It must be tough being a single mother. Thought I'd send her a present."

Cassie gave him a thumbs-up.

"How do you know she's single?"

"She told me. Said the father of her baby wasn't in the picture."

"When was the last time you saw her?"

Cassie raised her brows. Torrance was much too interested in Eva.

"Around about the time she went on maternity leave," Heath said.

"She hasn't contacted you since then?"

"There was no reason for her to. Why?"

"She seems to have disappeared."

"Disappeared as in 'into thin air'?" Heath asked.

"Pretty much."

"I don't know much about that kind of thing, but did you file a missing person's report?" Heath asked.

"No. She left her roommate a note, saying she was leaving. No reason for the police to look."

Cassie wrote a quick note to Heath: *Ask if they checked with her insurance to see if she's delivered.*

He repeated the question to Torrance.

"Nothing so far. I'm surprised at your interest."

Suspicious, Cassie decided. "End it," she mouthed to Heath.

"You know how narrow my world is," Heath said. "I enjoyed watching her blossom. Thought I would get a birth announcement when the baby was born and I realized I hadn't. Well, I won't take up any more of your time. Bye." He hung up before Torrance could say anything else.

"What do you think?" Heath asked.

"Something's not right. He wouldn't have continued the conversation otherwise. He might have referred you to the human resources director or Eva's immediate supervisor. He's taken a personal interest. He employs, what, fifty employees probably? He wouldn't normally keep track of someone that low on the organizational chart. Plus, we know he contacted Missing Persons."

"Doesn't prove anything."

"No." She drummed her fingers on the worktable, then she sat up straight. "Do you know for sure that she cashed your ten thousand dollar check?"

"I— No. Not for sure."

"Call your bank and find out."

"What good will that do?"

"I'm speculating."

Cassie wandered while he got the information. She was tempted to open his blinds but didn't, his office the last room in the house where they were still closed. Perhaps since she'd told him about the night-light, he might tell her why he lived in the dark.

"She didn't cash it," Heath said, hanging up the phone.

"Hmm."

"Hmm? That's it?"

"The other times you gave her money, was it checks or in cash?"

"Checks."

"She cashed those?"

"Immediately."

"Hmm."

"Cassie."

She came to attention. "Sorry. Let me think about this for a while."

"We need to check further into Brad Torrance."

"We need to find Eva," he said.

"Yes, but I think there's enough to approach him in person."

"Now?"

"Tomorrow."

"One more day, then."

One more day, she thought. "In the meantime, I'm going to make a visit to Child Protective Services, then head to the office for a little while. Okay?"

He set his hands on her shoulders. "You're sure they won't take Danny away?"

"Not a hundred percent."

A few beats passed. "You'll call me as soon as you leave there?"

"Absolutely. Don't sit here worrying. I have huge credibility with CPS. I've worked a lot with them. They know I intend to be a foster—" She stopped, swallowed. It showed how comfortable she was with him that she'd let that much slip. She hadn't told her plan to anyone outside the CPS office.

"I won't tell your boss," Heath said.

"Look, I'm all but licensed already. Background check is done. It's just a matter of issuing the license itself," she said defensively, hoping she was right. "And I have no plans to quit my job. I'll incorporate both somehow."

"You are really something."

He hauled her into his arms and kissed her, the way she'd wished all morning he would, with intensity and passion, changing the angle and deepening it, wrapping her even closer.

"Hurry back," he said.

"I will." She headed for the door, but stopped there and turned around. "Design me a house, why don't you. Something to hold maybe eight children ranging in age from ten to eighteen."

"Hard-to-place kids?"

He got it. "Bedrooms shouldn't hold more than two kids each," she said. "Big kitchen. Big dining room. A computer room. Could you do that?"

"I imagine so."

There, she thought as she left. That ought to keep him busy.

* * *

"So, CPS will let Heath keep custody for now?" Jamey asked when Cassie got to the office much later.

"As long as I'm in the picture. They don't know him, but they know me. They don't want to remove Danny from an environment he's thriving in, either." She leaned her elbows on her desk and rubbed her forehead, suddenly exhausted. Jamey sat across from her, not looking sympathetic. In fact he looked irritated. "You got a problem with that?"

"Nope."

"Yeah, you do. What's up?"

He held her gaze. "You're in too deep, Cass."

"I know."

"You're gonna fall, big—" He frowned. "You know?"

She nodded. "I don't live in fantasyland. I've known all along. And guess what? I'd do it again."

"You're in love."

"Yeah." The word came out as a whisper.

"You hardly know him."

"Crazy, huh?"

"Do you think he feels the same about you?"

The magic question. She knew Heath appreciated her. He'd become dependent on her in a way and yet was also amazingly independent. Since she worked in a take-charge kind of job, she'd started off as the dominant one—or tried to, she thought with a smile. He was no pushover just because he'd hidden himself from the world. *Chosen* to hide, according to him.

"What are you smiling about?" Jamey asked.

Her cell phone rang before she could answer. She pulled it out of her pocket. "Cassie Miranda."

"Hi, um, it's Darcy. You know, Eva Brooks's roommate. Remember me?"

"Of course." Her heart gave a little thump. "What can I do for you?"

"She called and wants to come get some of her stuff. I had the locks changed, you know, since she owes me money. I figured I wouldn't let her in until she, like, paid me?"

"Is she coming to your apartment?"

"Yeah. I told her to meet me after work. I thought maybe you could give her the papers, you know? Let her know she's got the money to pay me?"

Cassie paused. She didn't like misleading Darcy, especially since she was being helpful. "What time?"

"Five-fifteen."

"Great. I'll be there. Darcy? Look, I have to be honest here. I'm not really following up on an inheritance."

"Yeah, I figured."

Good. That made her job a lot easier. "Thanks a lot."

"Sure. Bye."

"Pay dirt," Cassie said to Jamey, then told him the plan.

"You can't kidnap her. Nor can you force her to talk. So, what does that leave?"

"I can play to her conscience, if she has one."

"What are you going to do?"

She picked up the phone and dialed Heath. She'd called him earlier, as she left CPS. "I have some more good news," she said.

"I could use some."

"Eva's roommate just called. Eva will be at her apartment in an hour."

"I'll be there."

She couldn't talk, she was so relieved that he would be coming.

"You there?" he asked.

"I'm here. You've got the address, right? I'll meet you there."

"Cassie." His voice got quiet. "This could be it. The end."

He would have to bring Danny with him. So much could happen. "The decision is yours, Heath."

His pause dragged out a few seconds. "It's time for the truth." He hung up.

"Okay," she said, placing her hands flat on her desk. "I'm going to get over there now and find a parking spot." She worried about him showing up, too, but she wouldn't tell Jamey that.

"Let me know what happens."

"I will. Don't worry so much, Jamey. I'm a big girl." She left in a hurry, not waiting for words of advice or wisdom. He couldn't tell her anything she didn't already know.

Nearly an hour later she saw Heath pull up in front of the apartment house. Directly in front of it. She got out of her car and slipped into the passenger seat of his.

"You couldn't have parked where she might not see you?" she asked, craning her neck to see Danny in his car seat. He was asleep.

"She won't recognize the car."

"She might recognize you through the windshield."

"You haven't seen her?" he asked.

"No." She touched his shoulder. "How was the drive?"

"Fine."

He might as well have told her to shut up. He had no intention of telling her if he'd been nervous or scared or whatever. She admired him for that.

"I'll do the talking," he said. "You can stand there and look…nannylike or something."

She laughed. "Should I put my hair in double braids?"

"Yeah. And act meek."

"Uh-huh." She grinned at him, enjoying the banter. "Like that's gonna—"

"Shh." He angled sideways, blocked his face by resting an arm on the steering wheel. "There she is."

She'd gotten her figure back in a hurry, Cassie thought. To look at her, no one would know that she'd given birth less than three weeks ago.

Heath grabbed the door handle.

"Wait. Let Darcy get here," Cassie said. "Eva needs to be inside the apartment so we can catch her there, see if she'll talk. Get Danny's car seat undone and ready to go. I'll watch for Darcy."

Two minutes later the black-haired, nose-studded woman arrived. By the time they got Danny and followed her up to the third floor, the apartment door was closed and an argument between the two young women filtered down the hall.

Cassie knocked. Darcy swung open the door.

"She's all yours," she said.

"What—?" Eva froze, her eyes wide. After a second she made a run for the door.

Even cradling Danny's car seat, Heath caught her and moved her back. Cassie shut the door, then leaned against it.

"Do you want to leave?" Heath asked Darcy.

"No way." She plopped into a chair and crossed her legs, bouncing her foot. "This I gotta see."

Tension cocooned them in expectant silence.

"Sit down," Heath said to Eva.

She did, although looking belligerent at the same time.

"I am not this boy's father," he said. "Who is?"

Fourteen

Heath watched Eva's eyes shift to the baby carrier, her expression mutinous. She was not going to make this easy on any of them—or herself.

Playing to whatever maternal instincts she had, he set the carrier on the floor close to her and crouched beside it, his hand on Danny's legs. He was aware of Cassie behind him, knew she probably didn't like him getting Danny close to Eva, but he was making the decisions this time.

Danny opened his eyes. He'd just begun focusing on Cassie and Heath if they got their faces close to him. He'd just begun to develop a personality all his own.... Heath drew a slow, quiet, calming breath.

"Look at this innocent boy and tell me how you could be so cruel as to deny him his father."

Her lips thinned even more.

"It's Brad Torrance, isn't it?" he said.

"Your boss?" Darcy screeched. "*Eeuw.* Icky."

"Isn't it?" Heath repeated.

Eva crossed her arms. "What if it is?"

"Have you been in touch with him at all? Does he know Dan— Does he know his son has been born?"

Heath waited. Her stony silence infuriated him. "How could you do that?" he asked, frustrated.

"You know what? It was easy. It was nothing."

"He deserves—"

"He's crazy! And his wife's crazier. You think I wanted to turn him—" she jabbed a finger toward Danny "—over to them?"

"So his wife knew about your affair? Knew the baby was his?"

"Affair?" She laughed, the sound hollow. "There was no affair. I was their surrogate. His sperm. Her egg."

Darcy gasped.

Heath sat back on his heels. He looked over his shoulder at Cassie. She gave no outward sign of reaction. Was she as angry as he, but just better at not showing it?

"They paid me," Eva said. "It was a *job*. I wasn't supposed to tell anyone, ever. It wasn't like it was an adoption or anything. It was really their baby."

"You said his wife was pregnant."

"See? She's crazy! She got this…*thing* to wear, to make her look pregnant. She could make it bigger a little bit at a time. She kept matching me." She shuddered. "Insane."

"But this child is theirs, Eva. You had no right not to hand him over. You had no right to deceive me, to let me think I was the father." *To let me love him, care for him, have hopes and dreams for him.*

"You know what?" She flung an arm wide. "You were the only sanity in my life during that pregnancy, that horrible, awful pregnancy. They started in on me right away. What I ate. How much sleep I got. Where I went. They micromanaged my life from the day the conception was verified. I was their possession.

"And then, *then* when I got to be about eight months along, they expected me to move in with them for the last month. Become their prisoner. No way. I would've suffocated. I was doing the job they paid me to do. I didn't have to give them more than that."

"Why didn't you cash Heath's check?" Cassie asked, coming forward.

"I took the check because I needed him to believe my story. I wasn't ever going to cash it." She started to cry. "I didn't know what to do. I got attached to him—the baby—right away. I hadn't planned on that. This tiny thing inside me, moving around, scaring me when he was quiet for too long, kicking me in the ribs, waking me up. I got attached, okay? I meant to tell you right away, Heath. I did. I was going to tell you when I left him with you. Let you give him to *them,* so I never had to see them again," she said plaintively. "But I saw the look on your face when you saw him and thought he was yours, and I chickened out. I didn't mean to hurt you."

"That doesn't account for the deception throughout the pregnancy. For telling me he was mine when he wasn't."

"I know. I'm *sorry.* They were just driving me crazy, but to them it was all about the baby. I was just a test tube or something. You treated me like a person. A special person."

So he was too nice to her? "Did you never intend to tell the Torrances that he'd been born and where he was? Were you going to disappear?" Cassie asked.

"I told them right before I came here."

Silence whooshed in, hot and desolate.

"I called them," she said. "They're probably at your house by now."

"You could be in serious trouble for what you've done," Cassie said when Heath couldn't put a sentence together.

"She's a P.I.," Darcy said, excited. "You'd better listen to her."

Eva zeroed in on Heath. "Look, I know what I did was wrong. The Torrances' craziness rubbed off on me. You would've gone nuts, too, I swear you would. But my intent when I started this was good. It wasn't about the money. Well, maybe a little, but not much. They gave me this sob story and I bought into it. She couldn't carry to term. They were in their forties. No time left. Yada, yada. I felt sorry for them."

Heath stood. Fury snaked through him. She could've saved everyone so much heartache. "Cassie, may I borrow your cell phone, please?"

"What are you doing?" Eva asked in a hurry. "Who are you calling?"

"What's Brad's cell phone number?"

Eva heard the tone in his voice and didn't hesitate for long. Heath dialed the number as she gave it.

"Brad, it's Heath. I've got your son. He's fine. He's healthy."

"He's got him," Heath heard him say. "Oh, God. He's got him. Where are you?"

"Are you at my house?"

"Yes, we just got here."

"Stay put. I'll bring him to you. It might take an hour, depending on traffic. But what I need to know now is if you want to press charges against Eva."

Fear ravaged Eva's face, as Heath intended. She would feel a little of what he had felt—and Cassie, and the Torrances. Tears poured from her eyes. She shook. Just then Danny started to cry.

"Is that my son?" Brad asked in a rush.

No, it's my son, Heath wanted to say. His heart fisted painfully as he said, "Yes. That's your son."

"Just bring him. Forget Eva. We just want our baby."

"Are you sure?"

"I'd like her to rot in hell for all the grief she caused us, but we want this kept quiet. Eva knows that. Leave her behind and come now, please."

"Okay." He ended the call and passed the phone back to Cassie. "You got lucky. Damn lucky. For now. And while he may not want to press charges, Eva, I still might," he added.

She reached into her purse and took out an envelope. He saw it was addressed to him.

"What's this?" he asked when she passed it to him.

"I cashed your other checks so you wouldn't be suspicious, but I kept the money to give back to you. It's all there. You were the best thing that happened to me during that time. Thank you for being so kind. Most men wouldn't have been."

The fight was starting to go out of him. "You've been hanging out with the wrong men."

"You're probably right."

He knew what he was going to do, but he didn't want to let Eva off too easily. He looked at Cassie. "Can we talk in the hall?"

She opened the door and stepped out. Heath followed with Danny, who had stopped crying.

"You're letting her go, scot-free," she said, her eyes cool.

He couldn't read her expression, but it didn't matter. He'd made his decision. "It's not scot-free. She has to live with what she did for the rest of her life."

"So do you."

"I'm angry, don't think I'm not. But I'm trying to think this through to the end, not just for the moment. In some ways I should be thanking her. She gave me the push I needed to start living again. And how much harm came from loving Danny? He changed my life." *He brought me you.*

The thought nested in Heath's mind, but this wasn't the time nor place to explore that revelation.

"It's up to you, obviously," Cassie said.

Heath slipped a hand around her neck and pulled her toward him. He kissed her hard, then he opened the door to return to the apartment.

"Since Brad is willing to let it go, I will, too," he said to Eva.

She folded into her herself and started to sob. "Thank you. Thank you, Heath. I'm so sorry. I really am."

He watched her for a minute, then he crouched in front of Danny's car seat and unbuckled him. He lifted him out. She'd gotten attached to him, but she'd still given him up. He gave her credit for that much. "Would you like to hold him?"

Her face was blotchy and tearstained, her eyes wide and filled with disbelief. Her nose was running. But she reached for Danny then tucked him close. "Hi," she said in a little voice. "I'm Eva. You lived in me for a while."

Darcy sprang out of her chair and threw her arms around Eva and Danny, tears streaming down her face. Heath glanced toward Cassie, but she was looking out the window. Her throat convulsed. His burned.

After a few minutes Eva put Danny back in Heath's arms.

"You need to apologize to Brad and his wife," Heath said.

"I know."

"Probably best to do it by letter."

She laughed, a shaky sound. "Okay."

He needed to get home, to do the next job, the harder one. He buckled Danny into his seat. Cassie said nothing as they walked down the three flights of stairs. When they reached the front door she said, "I'll follow you."

"All right."

She never looked at Danny. Never talked to him or put her face close and smiled at him. She'd already broken the ties.

Cassie saw the Torrances run across the yard as Heath pulled in ahead of her. She parked next to him. By the time she got out of her car, the couple had flung open the passenger door and were trying to figure out how to get Danny out of the car seat.

"Let me," Heath said gently.

Mrs. Torrance had her hands pressed to her mouth

and was crying. Heath set Danny in her arms. She cried harder. Danny joined her. Brad hugged them both.

Heath came closer to Cassie, but she couldn't look at him. She was filled with an emptiness so huge it echoed inside her, bouncing around, but like shards of glass cutting her up at the same time.

"I have clothes and…other things," Heath said.

"We have everything he needs," Mrs. Torrance snapped.

"Anna," Brad said softly. "He did nothing wrong. I'm sorry, Heath. We're just…emotional. We didn't think we would ever see him."

Heath nodded. He could only imagine their terror. "He does well on the formula you'll find in the diaper bag. If you want to know his schedule or anything else—"

"We'll learn it on our own, thanks," Brad said as his wife shook her head.

"I want to go home," she said.

"The car seat?" Heath pointed in the direction of the car.

"We have our own. Maybe I can call you later," Brad said.

"Anytime."

They started to walk away.

Cassie felt poleaxed. "We don't get to say goodbye?" she asked, her voice rising, panic gripping her.

The couple stopped and stared at her. Anna clutched Danny tighter.

"Cassie." Heath put an arm around her.

She shrugged it off. "After all we've done, we don't get that much?" She'd thought she could keep herself together, but she was unraveling so fast she couldn't even feel her legs. The emptiness in her was replaced by one huge, beating heart with cracks running through it. "Danny—"

Heath put both arms around her. "They have to go, Cassie. They need to take him home."

The couple walked away, gravel crunching beneath their feet, the sound excruciating to Cassie's ears. All the splits in her heart widened into red-hot fissures. She squeezed her eyes shut, struggled to breathe.

The noise stopped suddenly, then started again, getting louder, coming closer.

Anna Torrance stood in front of her and set Danny in her arms. "Say goodbye," she said, tears still fresh in her eyes.

Cassie didn't hesitate to gather him close. *Don't cry. Don't cry, don't cry.* She wanted to be able to see his face one last time, to memorize it.

"I love you," she said close to his ear, then pressed kisses all over his face. "You be a good boy."

She started to pass him to Heath, but he shook his head. He'd already let go.

"Thank you," she said to Anna.

"I don't even know who you are," the woman said.

"My name is Cassie." She put Danny in Anna's eager arms, took a step back, then another, deciding she couldn't watch them drive off. She didn't have a key to the house, though, so she headed around to the back. After a few minutes she heard them leave. Soon Heath joined her.

All he did was look at her and she fell apart. An inhuman sound came from her, low, keening, desperate. Then the tears fell, long, hot, endless streams of desolation. She pummeled his chest until he caught her wrists and stopped her, yanking her into his arms, imprisoning her there, holding her so tight she couldn't breathe. It didn't matter. She didn't want to breathe.

She didn't know this person, this Cassie, except that she acknowledged she wasn't just grieving for Danny but for her mother and her grandfather and her broken childhood, and she was grateful to be in Heath's arms.

He didn't hush her, didn't speak at all, but his body was like steel. After a long time, she relaxed against him. "I need a Kleenex," she said.

"Use my shirt."

She smiled a little. The muscles in her face still hurt. Had he cried? She didn't know. She angled back to see for herself. No. He hadn't. His face was lined with loss and pain but he hadn't found comfort in tears, as she had.

He kissed her, a long, tender, sweet caress, then held her close again, looking toward the west and the setting sun. With the land cleared they could see forever. It seemed apropos. The sun set as their chapter closed. It just shouldn't be so beautiful, she thought. But dark clouds were on the horizon, absorbing the color, in magenta and orange and a majestic purple.

Now what? Where to go from here? she wondered. Where did this leave her and Heath? She'd just let go of someone she loved. Could she let go of another one so soon?

"Let's go inside," he said.

She would have her answers.

Fifteen

The door to the nursery stood open. It was the first thing Heath saw when they entered the house. That and a pacifier looking achingly forlorn in the middle of the coffee table.

He didn't move. Neither of them did. Finally he said, "Go get in the spa tub in my bathroom, if you want. I'll join you in a few minutes."

She nodded, looking beat. He watched her trudge up the stairs, then he walked through the house, finding bits and pieces of Danny, evidence he'd been there. His bouncy seat, a burp cloth, a fluffy blue blanket. The damned pacifier. He tossed it all into the nursery and yanked the door shut. Empty baby bottles he threw out. A pediatrician's appointment on the calendar he x'ed out.

He didn't want Cassie to see any of it. He would wipe

out Danny's existence so she wouldn't cry anymore. He'd never heard anyone cry like that.

No, that wasn't true. Mary Ann had when Kyle—

He locked his fingers behind his head and stared at the ceiling. He was numb. Cold. Empty. And his penance wasn't done yet.

What was left? How much more punishment was there after being given another child to love, only to snatch him away? Take Cassie away, too?

He heard the water shut off upstairs. She would be waiting for him.

He schooled his expression as he went to join her, took off his clothes in his bedroom so that he could just slip in and not look at her face, not see the pain there.

She'd found a candle and brought it into the bathroom, leaving the lights off, making it easier to avoid looking in her direction. Was this it for them? The end? Had they forged the beginnings of something powerful or had it been as ephemeral as Danny's time with them?

"I could get used to this," she said as he settled behind her.

"To what?" *Me?*

"This tub. I think it's bigger than my entire bathroom."

It wasn't the answer he wanted, but what did he expect? They hadn't known each other all that long, and their relationship had grown out of one common interest, Danny. "You're a minimalist?"

"I'm a cheapskate. Plus I'm not there enough to need more."

"Yet you want a house big enough to hold a lot of kids." He leaned back, pulling her with him so that she rested against him. He didn't know how he could feel so lost and aroused at the same time.

"I've been saving. I'll get it, not too far in the future, I think."

He didn't want inane conversation. He wanted truth and reality—but he didn't want it until tomorrow. Tonight he just wanted Cassie.

He grabbed a bar of soap and worked up a lather with his hands then slipped them over her shoulders and down her breasts. She drew a quick breath and leaned more heavily against him.

"You're getting down to business," she said, her voice shaky.

"Pleasure." He wanted her. Needed her. She'd had tears as an outlet for her pain. Tears weren't an option for him. But holding Cassie, kissing her, making love to her—that would make his world tolerable again.

He whispered her name as he bathed her breasts leisurely. She groaned his name as he teased her with his palms. Her back arched as he used his fingers, drawing out her nipples, making them even harder.

He pushed a hand down her, between her breasts, down her stomach and beyond. A low sound came from her as he let his fingers delve and explore. His world turned hazy at the edges, but Cassie was in sharp focus in the center.

"Turn around." He wanted to see her face as he touched her.

Water sloshed to the edge of the tub but didn't quite spill out. The candlelight danced along her skin. There was a vulnerability he'd never seen before. Or maybe fragility, a word he never would have used to define her.

He stroked her skin, traveled the curves of her body with his hands, then his lips. She straddled him, bringing herself closer, wrapping her arms around his head and kissing him, her tongue hot, her mouth wet, her need obvious. She was sound and motion, earth and fire, contradiction and compromise. Her mouth slid to his jaw, then around his ear, down his neck, licking water drops. His skin rose in tingling bumps.

He put his hands on her head, stopping her as she reached his chest. He didn't want to relinquish control, not for a second, not yet. He was doing this for her pleasure first, only hers.

He eased her onto her back, lifted her arms onto the sides so that she could keep herself afloat as he pulled her hips higher and settled his mouth on her. She tasted of soap and Cassie, woman and want, present and future. Her heels dug into his back, raising herself even higher as he teased her, backing away, returning, backing away again. His thumbs made circles and dips, separating, searching, seeking what yielded the right sounds, sounds that told him she was headed for the point of no return.

The water churned as she moved her head from side to side, her hair floating sinuously around her head. He slowed down, made her gasp, made her reach, made her beg. There was nothing more important than her pleasure, nothing more urgent than to satisfy her need. He took his time in arousing her and found his own infinity in her gratification, loud and flattering and memorable then fading to a quiet aftermath of shudders and sighs.

Cassie lay there drifting, her eyes shut, her chest heaving until he pulled her into his arms. But she was still aroused and in desperate need of arousing him, satisfying him.

"Let's go to bed." She stood, held out her hand, clasped his. They toweled each other dry, went hand in hand into the bedroom. As they neared the bed she turned around, walking backward, enjoying the sight of him. He'd gained a little weight since she'd first met him, weight he needed. His hair looked even longer wet, yet there was no question that he was powerful and strong. Tempting.

She couldn't wait to get her hands—and mouth—on him.

She flung the duvet aside. Pushed back the bedding. Feeling like some kind of enchantress and not at all like herself, she put a hand to his chest and pushed. He let himself fall onto the bed.

"Be gentle with me," he said, his eyes sparkling.

"No way."

The sparkle became a hard glitter. She knelt beside him, leaned down to kiss him, let her hand trace a path from his chest to his thighs and back up again, not touching the hard, thick ridge of him but flying her hand just barely over, enough to feel his heat, enough for him to feel a breeze. He jerked up and groaned. She pushed him back down, thrilled with her own power.

"Cassie."

He said her name as if it were the last time, a question, a plea, a revelation. She wouldn't give in to it. She would take her time, take her pleasure, give him his.

"It's my turn," she murmured against his ear. "Don't move."

His hands fisted the sheet. Oh, yeah, power was good. She ran her fingers all over his body except where it counted most. He opened his eyes and, well, not glared, exactly, but gave her a look that told her she was wreaking havoc. She smiled and continued the torture until he grabbed her hand and flattened it on his erection, lifting up and groaning. She explored with her hand, testing his endurance, then she explored with her tongue, testing his control.

His voice lowered an octave as he uttered barely comprehensible words. She took him in her mouth, stopping all form of communication except movement. He didn't let her linger, though, but sat up.

"Stop," he whispered harshly.

"I'm not done."

"Yeah. You are."

He flipped her onto her back and plunged into her then stopped, buried deep, and made a low, guttural sound, his body unyielding. Then he moved, short, quick thrusts, his pelvis pressing hard into hers, his breathing ragged, matching hers. She wound her legs around him, pressed her heels into his thighs. The build to climax wasn't slow or gentle but fast and hard and staggering. They came together fiercely, wildly, mindlessly. No thought, just feeling, exquisite, memorable feeling. Then the inevitable descent that took forever but not long enough.

She curved her arms up his back, combed his damp hair with her fingers. Tears stung her eyes. Beautiful. He was beautiful. And breathtaking.

And it hurt so much that this would be her last night with him.

They fixed turkey sandwiches and ate them on the back porch while they watched the sky darken with black clouds, hiding the moon. The air smelled of impending rain, extremely rare for late September in San Francisco. Then after they went to bed the rain started to fall around midnight, no gentle, cleansing shower but a violent, pelting storm that rattled windows.

Neither of them mentioned watching Letterman. They left the blinds open and watched the rain and wind hammer the night. Heath had lit a fire in the bedroom fireplace earlier. Now he burrowed his face in her hair, caught the scent of his own shampoo and had no desire to be anywhere in the world but there in his bed, with her.

He didn't want to say anything to upset the tenuous peace of the evening. Neither of them mentioned Danny or the future. It seemed the best choice for the moment. Daylight would bring reality back with a vengeance.

But it left them with little to talk about. Exhaustion suddenly overwhelmed him. He needed to sleep, needed to empty his mind for a little while.

"Tired?" he asked.

"Very."

"Go to sleep, then."

She snuggled closer. A couple of minutes passed.

"You can turn out the light," she said.

He hesitated. "Are you sure?"

"I want to try."

He reached to turn off the bedside lamp and gathered her close again. The fire had died down to embers and offered little light. Without moonlight, the room was very dark.

He kissed her cheek, her temple, her forehead, then rested his cheek against her hair.

"My angel found me," she said, a smile in her voice. "Thank you."

He stayed awake until he knew she was asleep, then he joined her.

Sixteen

Cassie left her luggage by the front door where Heath would see it when he came downstairs. She'd gotten up early and packed. He'd continued to sleep. She waited in the living room, and waited and waited.

She knew the second he awoke. There was no noise to indicate it, but she knew. He didn't get into the shower but came right to the top of the stairs and stopped. She pictured him looking at her suitcases.

He came down, his tread measured, and walked into the living room. She stood. He'd pulled on a pair of jeans but that was all. She'd had her hands on that body, her mouth. She'd awakened him in the middle of the night by kissing his chest then moving down his body. "Ah, Cassie," he'd said in a gruff, excited, pleased way. "Where have you been all my life?"

She'd almost stopped, afraid of hurting him even more when she left in the morning, but unwilling to give up her last time with him.

Plus she'd slept all night without a light on.

Her fingers shaking now she shoved her hands in her pockets.

"You're leaving?" he asked, his voice neutral.

She nodded. *Because I love you. Because you're ready to go out into the world again, and your life is going to change. And because I would be a reminder of Danny, of more loss.* She knew he needed to do some living. He wasn't whole. He hadn't grieved, hadn't shared anything about Kyle with her. That was how she knew for sure that he wasn't ready for her.

It had been an illusion, the happy family. She was afraid, too, because illusions are so easily shattered. But mostly she wanted him to embrace life again.

"Why?" he asked after a long moment.

"My job is done." *I'm cutting my losses.* Surely he could understand that about her.

A total and instant change came over him. His expression turned icy. "I see. So, are you charging me for last night?"

She didn't plan on charging him for anything. Not one cent. She didn't know how she would work that out with her boss, but she would.

"No," she said. "I'm not."

"So it really was just Danny that kept you here. And some great sex. Been without for a while, have you?"

The bitterness in his words stung. "I don't want to hurt you—"

"That's a laugh."

"It's true. You may not understand it now, but I hope you will sometime." It was better to make a clean break now. If she lingered, he might see the truth behind her words. *I'm doing this for you,* she wanted to scream at him. *For you.*

Her stomach churned. She needed to go. Now. This instant. How had she let herself become so vulnerable? She'd gotten so good at preventing that.

She walked past him. "Goodbye, Heath." Grabbing her things she opened the door. She wouldn't look back at him. She wouldn't.

But she did. He stared straight ahead so she only saw his profile, saw how straight he stood, how his jaw flexed. It had been worse than she expected, leaving him. She'd thought she could have a conversation with him, but that would've been impossible. She had so much to thank him for, and yet she couldn't.

Live again, she told him silently. *Love again. I will always love you.*

She closed the door quietly, made her way to her car without running. She didn't feel his gaze on her as she had the first day she'd arrived. He hadn't gone to one of the windows to watch her.

Birds sang as she opened her car door. Sun bathed the house and yard, was reflected in the big glass windows. There was life here finally. Hope. A future. Things that had been missing the first day she arrived.

She would have to be satisfied with that. It could only get better from here.

Heath stood in the living room, his mind empty, staring at nothing. After a while he walked to the window. She was gone. Really gone. He'd been wrong about her.

No, not really, he decided. He'd known that Danny was the reason she'd come and stayed, but hadn't something else grown? He may not have been out in the world much lately but he didn't think he was that far off in his interpretation of action and words. And here he'd given her credit for honesty. Wrong again, Raven. Wrong again.

He fixed a pot of coffee then took a cup into the yard with him as he walked it. The rain had washed everything clean. Wet soil clung to his feet, dampened and muddied the hems of his jeans. He stood where he could see the city skyline. Was she home yet? Maybe she went straight to work.

His coffee had gone cold. He tossed the remains onto the ground, then turned on the garden hose to wash his feet. He took off his jeans on the back porch before realizing the door was locked, that he would have to walk naked to the front of the house.

Cassie would've laughed at him, her eyes sparkling. That laughter had filled his house with life. He'd been drawn to that first about her. Well, maybe not first but soon thereafter.

Stop thinking about her. He would. He had to.

He showered, stripped the sheets and washed them, not wanting her scent in his bed that night. He went into his office. Like he was supposed to work?

Automatically he booted his computer and brought up e-mail. Nothing critical. He looked at the various project names and decided he would find himself a mental challenge. The insurance center in Sacramento? The successful dot.com in Seattle in need of a larger building? The twenty-story structure in Los Angeles?

The dot.com, he decided, but as he went to click on the icon he saw the one next to it: Daniel Patrick. The digital photos he'd taken of Danny since the first day.

His finger on the mouse, he moved the arrow over the icon. After what seemed like hours he double-clicked on the folder. He read the list of contents and clicked on the first one, taken when Danny was hours old, asleep in his bassinet. Cassie hadn't even arrived yet. Heath stared at the picture. Danny had changed so much, no longer the red, wrinkly baby but a plumper, pinker one.

One by one Heath viewed the pictures. One by one he forwarded them to Brad Torrance's business e-mail address. Then he came to the last one, a picture he'd taken using the timer of Cassie, Danny and himself. He remembered the moment. They were outdoors. The background showed the cleared and tamed property and the view of the city and bay.

It wasn't Danny who had forced those changes in his surroundings, but Cassie. She'd pretended Danny was a little jaundiced and opened all the drapes and blinds. She'd forced Heath to look outside again. Danny was the catalyst, but Cassie was the instigator, sometimes subtle, mostly flagrant.

She'd barreled into his life, turned it upside down, then left. Fury blindsided him. How dare she? How could she toy with him like that? She had to know how much she meant to him. She'd have to be deaf, dumb and blind not to know.

Well, he could wipe her out of his life just as easily,

with one keystroke, in fact. She could walk out? So could he, in his own way.

His finger hovered over the delete key then froze there. After a minute it slid away, as if he had no control over it. He hit the print key, coded it for two copies, then hit Delete. He couldn't forward that one to Brad, and he didn't want it left on his computer, either. But he wouldn't wipe out the memory altogether, as had happened with Kyle.

He retrieved the two prints from the printer and stuck them in an unlabeled file folder then into his filing cabinet. He would never forget where they were.

Now that he'd purged the photos he would get down to work. He returned to his computer. Distracted he stared into space, but there was no space, no view, only a huge expanse of windows still covered by closed blinds. He got out of his chair, put a hand on the cord, then let his hand fall to his side. Not ready yet.

More determined, he sat again. He typed a command to open a file, but somehow it came out as "Kyle" instead of Kendall, the Seattle company. A file came up. A photo. One photo. Kyle.

He remembered it. He'd just gotten a digital camera to take to New Hampshire on their upcoming trip. He'd been experimenting with taking pictures and downloading them. The file wasn't on his screen usually but down where he would've had to scroll to it.

He hadn't seen it in three years.

Heath dragged his hands down his face, set them in his lap. His eyes lost focus. He drew a deep breath and clicked on the file. The photo opened. Kyle. Kyle with the laughing eyes, green like Heath's, and the blond, almost-white hair. He'd been singing "Itsy Bitsy Spider" when Heath snapped the picture. His hands were in the air making the motion of the spider climbing the water spout.

Heath put his hands on the monitor and traced his son's face—the impish smile, the white teeth, the jutting little chin. He ran his fingers over each eyebrow, the shell of each ear. His chest heaved, his breath stuck there. He leaned his cheek against the monitor, wrapped his arms around it, rocked back and forth. Tears flowed at last, at long last. Horrible, wrenching, racking sobs rose from him, the ugliest sound he'd ever heard. "Why not me?" he cried. "Why him? Why not me?"

He gave himself up to it, to the guilt, to the self-contempt, to the old arrogance that had been his downfall. He stormed around the office, slamming books, throwing whatever was handy against the wall until he finally fell to his knees and just grieved for the boy, for his son, for the light of his life, long gone dark.

Hours went by before he picked up the phone and hit a speed-dial button. He waited twelve rings. They didn't have an answering machine. He had to give them time to hear it, time to go indoors and answer.

"Hello?"

Just the sound of his voice resurrected the pain. Heath squeezed his eyes shut. "Dad?"

"Son? What's wrong?"

"I'm coming home."

Seventeen

Cassie stared out the picture window of the ARC conference room. The windy San Francisco Bay was dotted with boats and Windsurfers, normal for a Saturday afternoon. Quinn had called a meeting his first day back in the office after more than a month away on a trip that had taken him almost around the world, protecting a hotshot CEO with some international enemies. She wished she could do the same. Get away. Focus on work. Stop thinking about…everything.

"Last item on the agenda. We got a check from Heath Raven," her boss said, "but I haven't seen billing for him. He attached a note saying it was an estimate, but to let him know if he owed more or was due a refund."

Cassie felt Quinn studying her, and Jamey, as well.

"I didn't bill him," she said then turned around.

"Do you intend to?" Quinn asked.

She shook her head. "Send his check back, okay? I'll make it up to you. You can deduct it from my wages."

"Did you break rule number one, Cass?"

Never get personally involved with the client. She lifted her chin. "Yes."

"Was it the baby?"

"In the beginning."

He was quiet a few seconds. "If I don't let it go, it'd be like the pot calling the kettle black, wouldn't it?"

"Claire wasn't a client," Jamey reminded him.

"Close enough." Quinn stuck the check and letter back in its envelope. "Okay, Cass."

"Thank you," she said quietly, humbly.

"When did you see him last?"

"Ten days ago." Not that she was counting or anything. "I said goodbye."

"No hope?"

She shook her head. He hadn't even tried to talk her out of leaving. Not that she'd wanted him to or anything.

"Hmm."

Cassie frowned. "Why do you say it like that?"

"Because he called a little while ago, looking for you. I told him to come over."

"You what?" She pushed herself out of her chair. She couldn't see him. She couldn't. She was just starting to sleep at night again.

"He said he had some unfinished business." Quinn's cell phone rang. "That's probably him. I told him to call when he got here and I would unlock the door. Here—" he passed her the envelope "—you can return this."

He answered his cell phone as he left the room. "Be there in two seconds," Cassie heard him say.

She turned the envelope over and over. She needed to get herself under control. She couldn't let on how much she'd missed him, needed him. Wanted him. How she'd lost interest in the little things in life, like Letterman and food and sleep.

What unfinished business? She crushed the envelope in her fist. Why couldn't he have waited? It was too soon for him to be comfortable with his new life. He should take at least a year—

"You don't have to see him," Jamey said.

She looked at the crushed envelope. Where could she hide it? "I can't not see him. I'm weak."

He laughed. "Right. You are the strongest woman I know—who has a weakness for one man." He stood. "Don't jump to conclusions, Cass. Let him talk. See what he wants. He may surprise you."

"But in a good or a bad way?"

She heard his voice and she went weak in the knees. He preceded Quinn into the room, was introduced to Jamey, who then left, along with Quinn. The door was shut behind them. She tried to shift into her self-protection mode, the one that had helped her through countless situations before, but it refused to accommodate her. Her heart seemed to be on a marathon. She shoved the envelope under her just before he looked at her.

"Hello, Cassie."

"Hi."

"How've you been?"

She intertwined her fingers to keep from reaching for

him. "Fine, thanks. How about you?" *Inane prattle. Why are you here? What do you want?*

"I've been to hell and back, frankly. Can I sit down?"

"Sure." She straightened, curious. He didn't look bad. In fact he looked incredibly good. Some of the lines were gone from his face. And he'd cut his hair.

He didn't sit across from her but walked around the table and pulled up a chair next to her. He set a folder on the table.

"I went to see my parents."

"In New Hampshire?"

"Well, yeah."

"Why?"

"Because I needed to finally face losing Kyle."

She saw fresh grief in his eyes. It was all she could do not to hug him. "How did going home help you do that, Heath?"

His hands lay loosely in his lap. "About four years ago I designed a school for their community—my community, a private school that would serve a widespread area and be modern and comfortable, with central heat and air-conditioning, a computer lab, the works, although simple in many ways, too. They raised some of the money. I got them grants and donated the design. But I wanted to do more."

He paused. "I bought them a school bus so the kids wouldn't have to trek through the snow and rain during the winter."

Cassie went very still. *Bus accident. Kyle died in a bus accident.* "How were they getting to school?"

"Most walked. A few, a very few, were driven. The parents protested the gift. Didn't want it. Didn't need it. It hadn't hurt any of them as kids to walk to school. It wouldn't hurt their kids, either. When the snow is really bad, they stay home. No problem."

Cassie kept quiet, letting him tell her at his own pace.

"My ego was pretty big, though. Big-shot, successful architect, earning awards, making a name for himself, comes home to the commune and wants to improve their lives. I pushed and pushed and pushed until they finally accepted the gift. Arrogance," he said it like a curse word. "Unbelievable arrogance."

She couldn't help herself. She put her hands on his. She knew what was coming.

"Mary Ann, Kyle and I flew back for the opening of the school. Mary Ann was ticked that I'd pushed so hard for the bus, saying we didn't need to spend the money when they didn't want it, but I didn't let her have any input. Still, she came along, good wife that she was, but not on the bus ride. Kyle and I got on the bus at the beginning of the route so that we could welcome every student aboard. I was proud. I wanted him to be proud of me. 'Look what I did!'" He squeezed her hands. "A tire caught the lip of the road and the bus tipped. It slid down an embankment. Everyone survived except Kyle."

"Heath." She whispered his name in sympathy.

"I couldn't save him. He called for me in that last second, and I couldn't save him." He leaned closer to her. "You wondered why I wouldn't open the blinds in my house. It was part of my penance. I'd built that house for him and Mary Ann. We'd finished it just before we left on the trip and had only spent one night there. We didn't even have all the furniture in yet. I loved the view. I bought the property because of the view, designed the house to take advantage of it. I decided that part of my punishment was to live in the house…and not enjoy the view. This morning for the first time I opened the blinds in my office."

Cassie framed his face. "I'm so sorry."

"Thank you." He reached for her hands, taking them away and setting them in her lap.

She didn't know what to make of that. He didn't even want her to touch him? She reached for her brief-case, covering her confusion. *Why did you come,* she wanted to ask, *if you don't want me anymore?*

"What's this?" he asked, tugging the envelope from under her. He smoothed it out.

She felt her face heat. "We're returning your check."

"Why?"

"I can't bill you, Heath."

His gaze was intense, direct, all-searching, his eyes a deep forest-green, reminding her of his house, of the memories there, of her short time with him, then he blinked and changed his demeanor completely.

"I brought you something," he said, reaching for the folder.

She could see there was more in the folder, but he pulled out only one item and passed it to her. A picture of her, Heath and Danny. "Oh!" She ran her fingertips across the print, looked at him, then at the picture again. "Thank you. Thank you so much."

"I didn't know if you would want it, if it would only make it harder for you. I decided you would want to have it."

"Yes. Yes, thank you." She smiled at it. "He was such a sweetie."

"I've been in touch with Brad. He's doing well. They've given him a different name, of course. Do you want to know it?"

"No. Not now, anyway."

"Okay." He settled into his chair, his body relaxed, but his eyes sharp and focused. "You look beautiful."

He flustered her. She knew she looked worn-out, not beautiful.

"Have you been sleeping?" he asked.

She looked toward the view of the bay again. "Sure."

"Don't start lying to me, Cassie. Not now."

She met his gaze. "No, not well."

"Keeping the light off during the night?"

She shook her head. *No angel to kiss me good night.*

He eyed her in silence, then he reached for his folder and pulled out a sheet of paper, passing it to her. "You wanted a house designed."

Her heart raced as she took it from him. She studied it, her confusion growing by the second. "This is your house."

"With an addition."

"I don't understand." Did he want to sell her his house? Were there too many memories of Kyle there?

"We would call it Kyle's House," he said.

"We?"

He nodded. "It would be a haven, a place to feel safe. A place filled with noisy kids and laughter, as it was intended."

"We?" she repeated, her pulse thundering.

Leaning forward he took her hands in his. "I figured out why you left me so suddenly, so coldly."

"You did?"

"Because you love me."

Her eyes stung. "Doesn't make sense when you put it that way, does it?"

He smiled. "Not at first. I was angry and hurt, but eventually I came to realize that you wanted me to find myself. That's such a sixties' phrase, more suited to my parents, but it's true, isn't it? You wanted me to find myself."

"Yes." The rough, dry word dragged along her throat.

"And you figured once I found myself I wouldn't want you anymore."

"I wanted you to live. That's all I was thinking."

"I don't think that was all, but I'll let that go for now. You probably also think I couldn't possibly have found myself this quickly, that ten days is too soon."

She nodded. He was right. She did think that, even though a huge part of her hoped otherwise.

"Do I come across as a man who doesn't know his own mind?"

"No. Never."

"Then believe me when I tell you that I love you."

Her emotions had been close to the surface since he'd walked in the door. They began to spill over now. Her heart swelled, closing her throat, bringing fresh tears.

"I want to raise children with you, ours and any others who are sent our way. I found myself with you, Cassie."

"And Danny."

"Danny, too, but I've been able to make a place for him that no longer hurts. I helped him out during his first three weeks of life. Who knows what Eva would've done if I hadn't been there? And then there was you. Without Danny there wouldn't have been you."

She smiled. Her heart surged with love and hope.

"Can't you say the words?" he asked.

"I love you. I love you so much. I wasn't whole without you, either."

"Yet you sacrificed. For me."

"Yeah, well, I'm a helluva woman."

He laughed then kissed her finally, pulling her up so that they could hold each other close, feel their bodies touching. When the kiss ended and he held her against him, he said, "I'm going to visit the sites of all the buildings I designed but haven't seen in person. I'd like you to go with me. It will give us time together, time alone together. We'll figure out the rest of our lives."

"I'm in."

The words were casual, but the bright shimmer in her eyes told him how deeply she felt.

"You gave me back my life, Cassie. Now I want to give you yours. Something new and exciting. And permanent."

She looped her arms around his neck. "Happily ever after?"

"Shall I tell you how it'll be?"

"Please do."

"Okay. Once upon a time there was a beautiful princess, a cross between Rapunzel and Wonder Woman…."

* * * * *

*Don't miss the gripping conclusion of
Susan Crosby's miniseries*
BEHIND CLOSED DOORS
*with SECRETS OF PATERNITY,
coming in June 2005.*

™ **Silhouette**®

Desire®

presents the next book in

Maureen Child's

miniseries

THREE WAY WAGER

*The Reilly triplets bet they could go
ninety days without sex. Hmm.*

WHATEVER
REILLY WANTS...

(Silhouette Desire #1658)
Available June 2005

All Connor Reilly had to do to win his no-sex-
for-ninety days bet was spend time with the
one woman who wouldn't tempt him. Yet
Emma Jacobsen had other plans, plans that
involved a *very* short skirt and a change
in attitude. Emma's transformation had
Connor forgetting about his wager—but
was what they had strong enough to last
more than ninety days?

Available at your favorite retail outlet.

Coming in June 2005
from Silhouette Desire

Emilie Rose's
SCANDALOUS PASSION

(Silhouette Desire #1660)

Phoebe Drew feared intimate photos
of her and her first love, Carter Jones,
would jeopardize her grandfather's
political career. So she went to Carter
for help finding them. But digging up
the past also uncovered long-hidden
passion, leaving Phoebe to wonder if
falling for Carter again would prove
to be her most scandalous decision.

Available at your
favorite retail outlet.

COMING NEXT MONTH

#1657 ESTATE AFFAIR—Sara Orwig
Dynasties: The Ashtons

Eli Ashton couldn't resist one night of passion with Lara Hunter, the maid at Ashton Estates. Horrified that she had fallen into bed with such a powerful man, Lara fled the scene, leaving Eli wanting more. Could he convince Lara that their estate affair was the stuff fairy tales were made of?

#1658 WHATEVER REILLY WANTS…—Maureen Child
Three-Way Wager

All Connor Reilly had to do to win his no-sex-for-ninety-days bet was spend time with the one woman who wouldn't tempt him. Yet Emma Jacobsen had other plans, plans that involved a *very* short skirt and a change in attitude. Emma's transformation had Connor forgetting about his wager—but was what they had strong enough to last longer than ninety days?

#1659 SECRETS OF PATERNITY—Susan Crosby
Behind Closed Doors

Caryn Brenley and P.I. James Paladin had a son without ever meeting face-to-face *or* skin-to-skin. When Caryn learned James was her child's sperm donor, she reluctantly agreed to let father and son meet. James jumped at the opportunity, but pretty soon he wanted to get close to Caryn—the natural way.

#1660 SCANDALOUS PASSION—Emilie Rose

Phoebe Drew feared intimate photos of her and her first love, Carter Jones, would jeopardize her grandfather's political career. So she went to Carter for help in finding them. But digging up the past also uncovered long-hidden passion, leaving Phoebe to wonder if falling for Carter again would prove to be her most scandalous decision.

#1661 THE SULTAN'S BED—Laura Wright

Sultan Zayad Al-Nayhal came to California to find his sister, but instead ended up spending time with her roommate, Mariah Kennedy. Mariah trusted no man—especially tall, dark and gorgeous ones. True, Zayad possessed all of these qualities, but he was ready to plead a personal case that even this savvy lawyer couldn't resist.

#1662 BLAME IT ON THE BLACKOUT—Heidi Betts

When a blackout brought their elevator to a screeching halt, personal assistant Lucy Grainger and her sinfully handsome boss, Peter Reynolds, gave in to unbridled passion. When the lights kicked back in, so did denial of their mutual attraction. Yet Peter found that his dreams of corporate success were suddenly being fogged by dreams of Lucy….

SDCNM0505